Rejected to Accepted

Catherine Marie Calvetti

PublishAmerica
Baltimore

First printing

ISBN: 1-60441-811-7
PUBLISHED BY PUBLISHAMERICA, LLLP
www.publishamerica.com
Baltimore

Printed in the United States of America

Dedication

I dedicate this book to all people who have felt crushed down, beaten up, and worthless. May you find hope in the only answer to all of life's questions: Jesus Christ, Lord of all.

Acknowledgments

First of all I want to acknowledge Jesus Christ, my Lord and Savior, who gives me the courage and inspiration to live life to the fullest by letting go of the past and trusting Him with everything.

May You be glorified.

My mother for giving me your very best, never giving up on me and showing me that good will always conquer bad.

I love you.

My dad for taking me in and making me yours.

I love you.

My husband who accepted me as I am, lovingly and patiently letting me become all that God has called me to be.

Thank you.

My friends Donna, Carmen, Patty and Wanda who have supported me from the beginning, encouraging me to get my testimony onto paper so others can be healed.

I could not have done this without you.

Chapter 1

I, Shelby Elizabeth Smith, did not come into this world the acceptable way. My 21-year-old mother was the youngest of seven children and unwed. She was the daughter of a hard working Scottish immigrant father and a 1st generation American-Bohemian mother. During the time she found out she was going to have me she also found out her mother had terminal cancer and would be gone before my birth. My grandma made it to her fifty-third birthday in March but never met me, her twelfth grandchild, born the last day of spring 1961.

Against the social norm and advice of friends and family my mother decided to keep me and raise me on her own. The relationship with my biological dad was rocky, at best. There was a woman that worked with my mom, at the same mill, who claimed that her baby was his too. He married the other woman, but that relationship was short lived and quickly ended in divorce. He re-enlisted in the Air Force and started a new life in Kentucky, abandoning both of his children. The seed of rejection was planted in my life and would affect me for many years.

I do not know much about my mother's early struggles as a single mom. I do know that all of her six siblings had moved out of the state of Minnesota. The eldest, Diane, had recently moved back and lived only fifteen miles away. Diane was married to a doctor. Howie was the attending physician at my birth and actually delivered me. He spent a lot of time with me, stating that I was the most beautiful baby he had ever seen. His favorite hobby was taking photographs, and I was one of his most preferred subjects. From all the photos he took it looks like I was a very happy baby.

I was baptized July 1961 at Saint Peter's Catholic Church. My mom's brother George and a friend of hers from work became my godparents. My mom made sure I had the best spiritual roots she could give me.

My mother continued working in the mill. At some point she met a man named Kendrick. He had just finished a stint in the Marines and was recently divorced. He owned a small-engine repair shop in the neighborhood my mom grew up in. One day she and a friend stopped in to see if someone could fix her dad's broken lawnmower. Kendrick was just the man to fix the machine, but not one to pass up an opportunity. He started talking and asked her out on a date. Their relationship progressed quickly from there.

In early June of 1962 they married. It sounds like they had a very rocky start once the marriage vows were said. We moved from rental to rental every few months for the first few years. Wanting to provide a home for us, Kendrick decided he would use his gambling skills to get some extra cash. He showed up one night at the little house we were living in with enough money from a poker game to make a down payment on a house. Our new dwelling was a four-bedroom home in a nice neighborhood only three blocks from where Grandpa lived.

From what I have gathered Kendrick's family was not very happy that he had married an unwed mother, this was just not the norm in the sixties. Since his folks lived over two-hundred miles away they were not part of our everyday lives. We only spent time together when we traveled up north or they came to southern Minnesota by us. I never really bonded with my new grandparents. Grandma died when I was five years old. Grandpa could not stay by himself, so he came and lived with us for a short while but then was put in a nursing home until his death a few months later.

Beer and alcohol always seemed to flow freely in our home and just about anyplace we went. One of my first sentences, according to my baby book, was, "Do you want a beer?" From the photos and statements in my baby book I liked to drink beer whenever possible as a toddler. I was told that one day I finished off my grandpa's bottle of ale, ran over to my aunt, and said, "Grandpa wants another beer." I was only three at the time.

My mom really wanted more children; she wanted to have a big family like the one she grew up in. She and Kendrick found out after several medical tests that they could not physically have any children together. At first Mom was devasted. It was not very long afterward though that she found out that Susan, my biological father's niece, was pregnant with twins. Susan knew she was unable to raise these children by herself so she offered the babies to my mom for adoption. My mom was very excited to be able to have two more children so quickly, so she started legal procedures right away. At court the judge called my mom into his chambers and heartily discouraged this adoption. He felt that since the mother of the babies knew my mom it would cause many future problems. This adoption did not materialize, but the judge helped my mom start the paper work through the state of Minnesota to adopt an anonymous baby. It was not very long after that a letter arrived stating that a baby boy had been put up for adoption, and if they wanted we could bring him home and make him part of our family.

I was not allowed at the initial visit, but several weeks later Brody came to live with us, and he became my brother. My mom desired to have an even larger family, so my parents decided to try taking in foster kids. For a while we had a brother and sister, ages four and five. Because my parents were unable to handle all the problems that these two abused children brought with them, plus the care of a toddler and a baby, Polly and Otto had to be sent on to another home. This was heartbreaking for my mom but she just concentrated on being the best mom she could be trying to work through all the emotions of not being able to help those kids.

I don't recall many of the details, but I do remember there seemed to be some kind of turmoil that was going on during those times. Kendrick drank, gambled and womanized. When I was young I could not understand why my mom was upset so often. She was careful to try to hide the discord from us kids. I am sure the chaos had a lot to do with the way their relationship was defined on a dominant, submissive level, cultural communication norms, and my mother's desire to avoid conflict as much as possible.

Chapter 2

My mom was a stay-at-home mom for my first seven or eight years while Kendrick continued to run the repair shop. She did many great things with us kids, making sure we had dance, swimming and piano lessons, were involved in the library program and scouts. She was always making something artsy and taught me how to do many different kinds of crafts. She also is quite the giver and taught me how great it is to bless others by giving whenever possible to charities, neighbors, and the less fortunate.

I was a very quiet kid in school. Kindergarten was very frightening for me; my class was held in the basement of a huge old school; it was actually the one my grandmother, mother, aunts, and uncles had attended. It was hard to leave my mom, baby brother, and home to go to that school each day.

First grade is just a blur but, I do remember parts of second grade. During that year our whole school moved into a new building in another part of town. It was not complete when we moved in. I still remember the fear of not having doors on the bathroom stalls, but I am not sure if it really happened or I was just afraid it would.

One of the good memories from that era in my life is when our class wrote letters to the president of the United States, we were each sent a booklet about the White House in return. It really made me feel important that someone of such notoriety would acknowledge me. As a child I did not realize that the president himself did not send it, but it was from his publicity office.

My maternal grandfather also supplied many happy days. He faithfully picked my brother and me up each school day in his

Studebaker making sure we arrived safely at school. He was always there for me providing trips to Lake Windigo for a swim, dilly bars from Dairy Queen, and cookies after school. He gave me many thoughtful gifts from my first bike to a play-by-number organ, but most of all he had time for me; he listened and taught me much. Education was very important to him since he was never able to get a formal one and had to quit when he was only ten years old to help with the family farm. He taught me about the seasons and the planets, and a little Scottish and U.S. History. He was always making sure that my mind was challenged and never idle.

I attended Catechism classes at the Catholic Church where I had been baptized. I was being prepared to take my first communion. Something I learned at the class devastated me. I was informed that my parents would not be allowed to take the Holy Sacrament with me. According to the Church rules at that time they were considered unforgivable sinners, he being divorced and she marrying him. The rejection of my parents by the Church confused me and hurt me deeply. I just could not understand why they could not partake in the Lord's Supper. At this time in my life I felt the Church was the same thing as God, so I began to form an opinion that God was a very judgmental being whose job was to point out all that I or my parents did wrong and punish us for it. If God rejected my parents He must think that I am even lower in status than they and my reasoning was that He must be rejecting me too. Those seeds of rejection were continually being planted, growing and entangling my life.

Another unhappy event from my First Communion had to do with my dress. My mother was told that none of the girls were going to wear those beautiful mini bridal dresses. She was informed to just save the money and get me a plain regular white dress, so she did. I ended up being the only girl in my whole class without a fancy dress. This did not help my already low self esteem and made me think that I was not worthy to wear a beautiful dress like the other girls.

One day my parents started a new adventure together. They bought the bar where they had their first date, right next door to the small engine repair shop. I learned many life lessons in that place, like not to argue with a drunk, the customer is always right (even if they aren't), it is a good idea to stay within sight of other adults, dirty old men can make you feel very uncomfortable, and potato chips, candy bars, and soda can fill an empty stomach.

I do recall a couple friends from third grade that I stayed in touch with through Brownies but never really saw outside of that. Fourth grade was a whole new nightmare. My parents decided I needed to go to a parochial school. Now I had a variety of things to learn, a different building to find my way around, faces and names of teachers and classmates, the rules I needed to know, the rules about going to confession weekly and the regulations for taking the Holy Sacrament of Christ's Body since I would now be attending a church service each morning. I also needed to try to make new friends, something I was not very good at, as I was very shy.

Oftentimes our phone would ring before six in the morning. When it did we knew it was the police letting us know that the tavern had been broke into and burglarized. The newspaper put in one of the police reports that the thief had found money hidden a cigar box. From that point on every time we were robbed the boxes of cigars were all dumped out on the floor.

One time when our family returned from a trip up north we found out our house had been burglarized. My brother, who was around five years old at the time, went to his bedroom. As he flipped on the light he saw a man crawl out the window. He screamed, and our parents went running to see what was wrong. The window was open and footprints were found in the dirt below, but no one else saw the thief.

Also during this time the shop was broke into. The team of burglars broke through a cement block wall and then got into the safe. The bandits stole the guns and money out of the safe. A few weeks later they broke into the local high school. As they burglarized the school the police were notified and promptly arrived on the scene. One of the men shot and killed a police officer with the weapon they had stolen from my dad.

Once again I try to get good memories to surface from this time in my life, but mostly unpleasant ones pop into my mind. One that humiliated me and really sticks with me was at the beginning of fourth grade. That day we started a new art project I misunderstood the directions and did not place the magazine clipping of Big Bird correctly on the paper. I guess he was supposed to be camouflaged into the surroundings but I just hid him in a tree. My teacher humiliated me in front of the whole class, bringing my error to everyone's attention. This just added to my feelings of being out of place and lonely.

At least I made a friend in fourth grade—Holly, the tenth of fourteen kids. We found out we had a few things in common besides our age and religious training. Our middle names were the same, both our moms worked, our dads drank a lot, and both dads had been married before. I always thought it would be great to have a sister, and watching Holly with seven sisters, I saw the good and the bad of sibling relationships. Even though at times I was envious that Holly had so many sisters to share time and clothes with, I did not think it would be fun to share one bathroom with that many people.

A life-altering tragedy that happened in my childhood was in fifth grade. A girl my age died of an aneurysm. She had been in my Brownie Troop when we were younger, but I had lost contact with her when I switched schools. It was very hard for me to understand why God would allow her to die and made me wonder if I would die suddenly like my friend.

During the next few years I learned more about the effects of alcohol than I ever wanted or needed to know at that age. My dad showed up at school under the influence and chewed out one of my teachers. If there was a reason, I do not remember what it was. I just know that I was embarrassed beyond measure.

My parents obtained another bar, this one out on Lake Windigo, causing them to work even more long hours. I spent most of my weekends and free time at the bars, and if I wanted to see my mom after school I would walk over to the tavern. It was only a couple blocks away. I usually walked to Grandpa's house, where Brody and I and sometimes Holly would have cookies and milk, visiting with Grandpa until mom got off of work. She would take us home, quickly make supper, and go back to the other bar to work the night shift. This did instill a strong work ethic in me.

Over the years we had a few really terrific babysitters who were fun and great to be around. We started reaching the age when we didn't think we needed a babysitter anymore, and the parents decided to try it. I do remember getting scared during a few storms and calling my mom on the phone crying in fear but mom could not come home because she was working. I am sure that was very hard on my mom too.

Kendrick's bachelor half-brother, Maurice, moved into our basement during this time. He had been living in New York City, but had retired and decided to come back to Minnesota. My parents thought this would be nice; they would not have to get a babysitter or worry about us being home alone unsupervised. Little did they know that Maurice did not like kids very much.

One time he pulled the chair out as I was going to sit on it, sending me right down onto the floor. I bruised my tail bone. He thought it was a funny practical joke. Uncle Maurice had a short fuse, too, and would hit my brother and me over the slightest thing; we usually had no clue why we got the beatings. The time I remember the most vividly was the night he dragged me across the floor by my hair. My brother tried to help me by pulling me in another direction, which just caused more pain and bruises.

It took me some time, but I eventually told my mother; who mustered up the courage to tell Dad. At first he would not believe that his brother would hurt us kids. All I remember is that there was much screaming and yelling going on, and my mom told me to go take a bath so I could calm down and stop crying so hysterically. While I was in the tub she sent my dad in to see all the bruises. I am not sure what was more humiliating, the beating or having my dad see my naked body at eleven years old. Mom, Brody, and I went and stayed at Grandpa's for a few days. The bruises healed, and the pain left, unlike the emotional wounds from the words that pierced deep within me and festered for years.

I reached the age where I wanted to start earning a little spending money, so I started going door-to-door selling Christmas cards and homemade ornaments. I also began babysitting for two different families.

Our family dog Heidi, a red, short-haired Dachshund, had to be put down at this point in my life. She had been around my whole life and was very dear to me. It was a heart-wrenching experience to say goodbye to one of my best buddies.

At the end of seventh grade our parents informed Brody and I that we were moving over two-hundred miles north to run a resort. It had been built by Kendrick's ex in-laws, but they had sold it to someone else a few years prior to this time. The whole thing was a shock to me. Not only was I going to have to learn a whole new school again, I was moving into a different culture, from the busyness of the city to a desolate tiny community in the middle of the woods. I was leaving my best friend Holly, my grandpa, babysitting jobs, and the life I was familiar with. I have no idea why they decided to move or even if it was a consensus between the parents. They did sell the engine shop before the move.

Chapter 3

The first summer in Heron Creek was a busy one, the resort had twenty-five overnight cabins and six housekeeping cottages. Mom and I washed all the sheets in a ringer washer, hung them out on the line to dry, and then ran them through a mangle to press them smooth. It was hard work, but it kept me from getting too lonely. We had plenty of company coming up from the city to check out the place and get a "free" vacation, which added to our work load. Best of all, Grandpa and Holly visited numerous times.

I quickly picked up a couple babysitting jobs so I could have a little spending money. There were no real stores for nearly twenty-five miles: only touristy shops, a Five and Dime and a General Store, that took quite a bit to get used to.

The first day of Eighth grade was more of a challenge than I could have ever imagined. It was the first time in my life I ever had to ride a school bus. The bus dropped us off in front of a school after a very long ride through winding roads in the woods and then finally into the middle of town. I followed the kids into the nearest school building. I located where the eighth grade was and proceeded to the class room. Once I was seated the teacher asked who I was, I told her, and she informed me that I was not on the attendance list, so I needed to go to the office. I went to the office and told the secretary all the information she needed to get me registered and then I went back to class. A short while later the secretary came and got me she informed me that I was in the wrong school, and that I needed to go down the street to the Catholic school, so off I went, not realizing I was headed the wrong way.

After wandering around town for a while and ending up by the little shops, I headed another direction. I eventually noticed way down the street the church that my parents had taken me to a few times. I promptly headed toward that. It took me some time to find the right door for the building and locate the place I was supposed to be. There were about sixteen kids in the class, half seventh grade, half eighth, another big culture shock for me and an embarrassing way to meet them. Sister Mary Robert, my new teacher, got me situated right away.

The resort was not winterized, so the cabins had to be closed for the winter. This meant there would be no money coming in all winter, so Dad had to find work. He took a job driving truck for a potato farm. We still did not have much, eating mostly potatoes and homemade sauerkraut.

I had a hard time adjusting to life in the north woods, so when winter came and I was complaining of feeling sick, my parents felt that I was faking to get out of school. They said I had to go to school since I did not have a fever. Each morning after the long bus ride we went to mass first thing. Almost every day I would get very sick and have to run to the basement bathroom during the service where I would vomit and then lie on the floor to let the coolness help me pull myself together. During this time my mom was sick a lot too, and we thought it was probably the flu. One time while decorating for Christmas I was hanging something up high and passed out and fell, landing on the couch. Something was wrong. Around this time my mom was taken to Saint Paul and hospitalized to try to find out why she was so sick. Grandpa came up to stay with us and help around the house. While he was there he became sick; even our dogs and cat were ill. Thinking it was the flu we kept on going continuing our daily routines as best we could. It did not seem to affect Dad much, but he was gone most of the time driving truck. When Mom returned she was feeling a bit better, but as soon as she walked in the door her head felt like it was going to explode, and she said she could smell gas. I know it is impossible to smell carbon monoxide, but Minnesota Public Service came over within minutes, and that is what it was. The furnace had been converted from coal to gas and was not vented properly. We were all being poisoned from the carbon monoxide. It was a miracle that we survived.

Even though part of me did not like going to church six times a week I found solace in a painting above the front of the altar. That painting portrayed the story from the Bible where Peter had stepped out of the boat. He was reaching for the Lord's hand while waves crashed all around him, and I could relate to that feeling, as I was in a tumultuous life, and I was reaching for something, yet whatever it was seemed just out of reach.

That year I ended up needing my tonsils and adenoids removed. That was not the only medical procedure I needed; I also had some type of acne treatment that was horrid. The doctor had me hold hot cloths on my face, then cut the pimples open, drain them, and apply medicine that stung as much as my tears did. I felt physically miserable most of the time and mentally guilty for running up medical bills. My dad mentioned the outrageous cost of the hospital bill. He was upset about it, and I took his anger personally.

Mike, a guy who I had met on the school bus, was one year older than I. He befriended me and shared how his dad had recently died from some painful disease. We became good pals, spending time together. He was a shoulder to cry on. We dated others, but could count on each other to be a listening ear. I think he may have wanted to be a bit more than friends, but we never became romantically involved. I did like going to his mom's house and having dinner there. I could sense a peace there that I could not describe. She always had religious shows on the television. She daily watched "The 700 Club" and "The PTL Club." She seemed to enjoy them, but Mike and I always made fun of them.

One time that spring, I went along on the weekly dump run with my dad. As we drove in I noticed there was a pile of food, wheelbarrow high, that someone had just thrown out from their freezer. Since it was still partially frozen I begged my dad to bring some of it home, but he refused. After a winter of potatoes and sauerkraut I just could not understand why we could not take the food.

The day-to-day routine was usually full of turmoil. Kendrick was driving truck, and when he got home he demanded that there better be a cold beer in front of him before his rear hit the chair. Most days that was my responsibility to run to the refrigerator in the recreation room, that was designated just for beer. It was in a separate building. I found it easier to bring two or three at a time so I would not get in trouble. I was also expected to scratch his back for a while every night. He was unhappy and always seemed to be looking for something to argue about. When Mom would do something one way he would be upset about how wrong that was, so the next time Mom would do it the opposite way, and she would get berated on how it was supposed to be done the way she had originally done it.

Our home was always filled with a lot of tension. They had lost respect for each other. The hurtful words that would be said were so painful I would do just about anything to try and avoid them. Dad would say things like, "You are useless, and I wish I would have raised pigs. At least then I would have gotten some meat out of the deal." He always called me "Lazy Lizzy" and let me know how my body type was not like a real woman. He did not realize how this "teasing" actually ate away at my self esteem and made the ever-growing rejection within me increase. He swore often and talked unkindly about other people all the time. Sunday mornings were always filled with much turmoil as we got ready for church, all the way there and all the way home. This behavior made me question the whole reason for going to church. Were we going to earn some type of brownie points with an uncaring God who is hard to please, or were we going to learn more about God? I could not tell.

At this point in my life I just wanted to escape from reality so I spent a lot of time either in my bedroom listening to music, hiking in the woods, or working at the local grocery store. I helped run the bakery, learning how to fry donuts and bake.

I usually kept quiet and to myself, but as my teen years started so did some rebellious ideas. I thought it would be good to let my dad know of the hypocrisy I was witnessing. One night I really messed up. I broke our family rule that children should only speak when spoken to. That evening the president was giving a speech on TV. I rolled my eyes and made a comment that was not appropriate, showing disrespect to someone in authority. Dad was drinking, so it escalated into a full-blown screaming fight, as usual. This just added fuel to my growing desire to get out of the house.

Dad did not drink alcohol when driving semi; however, he would drive cars and even run chainsaws under the influence. One afternoon he attempted to cut down a tree that was hung up on another; it snapped back and ripped off his ear. My mom had to take him into the emergency room to get it sewn back on. Even though I was feeling the need to separate from my parents I still loved them and did not want to see them get hurt. I really cried and worried when Dad hurt himself.

It is miraculous that he was never in a drunk-driving accident; he did receive several tickets for driving under the influence. Being drunk and getting others drunk was one of Kendrick's pastimes. He didn't care what people he served alcohol to, he just liked seeing them looped, from little old ladies to guys who drove motorcycles, hung drywall, or cleaned carpet. He even offered liquor to priests—his best wines, of course. I think it somehow made him feel better knowing that these "men of God" were not perfect either. Other times he would have young men in their twenties over. Some of them were guys he drove truck with, others lived at the resort in the housekeeping cabins. He often had me supply the full beer bottles or pour brandy in the glasses. The guys would notice me and make me feel good by saying kind things to me. I learned that even though I did not think much of myself I could get attention from guys, something I began to think was the way to love and acceptance.

Ninth grade I was back in a public school. The building was very old but new to me. At least none of us freshmen knew our way around the building. Being back in a public school with many more kids made it easier to get lost in the crowd but still very hard to make friends. Most of these students had known each other since kindergarten and weren't about to let some city kid in on their friendships. Searching for love and a place to belong I clung onto the first guy that showed me attention. The relationship stayed very innocent, but when he broke it off the rejection crushed me. Soon I began to entertain thoughts about suicide and turned inward going straight to my room each night after school to dwell in my pitiful thinking that death would be better than this.

One time I actually took a knife to my wrist and was about to cut, but as I tried to "cry out" the pain, a thought came to me that maybe, just maybe, there was someone out there that would love me, a father, a sibling, someone, anyone. I turned my record album up on the phonograph using the headphones to help me escape into the music long enough to take my mind off the pain.

I also found other methods of escape during this time in my life, things that were illegal and I am ashamed of, but were a part of my life. Funny thing, it was the daughter of friends of my parents who got me to try drugs first. Since there was a constant influx of friends from the city who came up to vacation at our resort I was always exposed to new people. One of the friends was a fellow bar owner who came up with his two teenage kids to escape their mother for a while, since they were divorcing. Even though the eldest girl was a straight-A student she smoked pot and told me all about it and asked if I had tried it.

Afraid to be rejected by her I said, "Oh sure!" I was relieved to find out she did not have any with her. Several weeks later, though, I was allowed to stay at her house when we were down for a visit. One of the first things she did was pull out a joint, and I was too embarrassed to tell her I had never tried it before. I did not want to be rejected by her. I was glad I had been sneaking my parents cigarettes for years, so inhaling was not too hard for me. My parents never realized that encouraging this relationship was not a good idea; they were clueless that this gal did drugs.

I continued to search for God, but He seemed elusive. I do remember something that happened around this time. I was sitting alone on the dock overlooking Thunder Lake. I dared to pray, "God, if you really exist, show me." Although the sky was filled with clouds, an area suddenly broke open where I could see the blue sky and sunshine high above. I felt something deep inside say that was a glimpse of heaven. It really touched me, and I remember trying to describe it to my art teacher, as I wanted to draw or paint what I saw. I told him it was like I was sitting inside a clear beach ball and then looking up into heaven. He listened, but I never did get that image captured on paper. Being out in nature gave me a sense of peace and knowledge of a divine creator.

School was a way to keep my mind off the commotion going on at home. Another way of escape for me was listening to music, which also gave me a false definition of love. As I continued to search for love I set my eyes on a man nine years older than me. He was living in one of the cabins at the resort, and I figured I could win him over by showing him how much I cared for him. I dreamed he would be my knight in shining armor who would marry me and help me escape the hell at home. I would go to his little place as often as I could to clean for him. I spent hours washing the dishes, cleaning the floors, and just being in his presence. I pushed aside the words when he told me he was seeing someone else. I continued to make myself available to him. I decided to create the song, "Tonight's the Night," sung by Rod Stewart and succeeded, although it was not quite as wonderful as the song made it out to be.

I was always trying to be good, or at least my parent's definition of good. I attended Catechism class every Wednesday without complaint, yet many questions were swimming in my head. I tried to follow the ever-changing Catholic "rules," but they confused me. I did not understand why such things would change as much as they did. Why could the wafer not touch my teeth? Why could only the priest touch it? Why could I all of a sudden be good enough to have it placed in my hand? How could someone other than a priest now hand it to me? I really wanted to know and even tried to read the Bible myself, something I had to hide from my parents, as I felt they would be upset with me if I did. Why all these rules, yet it did not seem to matter how people behaved? One night I got brave and asked my Catechism teacher who Adam and Eve's children, Cain and Abel, married. I remember being shunned for such a foolish question.

One time I attended a weekend retreat at the church just for teens; it may have been part of my confirmation class. Father Bruce, a Jesuit priest, surely a man who knew God, was someone I wanted to get close to. I felt like the priest was Jesus himself, but I believe my hormones and lack of knowledge of true love caused me to develop a crush on him. Of course I never let him know what was going on in my mind, this silly puppy love feeling. He left after the weekend and visited the church one in a while. I quickly gave up that crush realizing how ridiculous it was. Sadly he, the motorcycle priest, died a tragic death from huffing many years later.

There was a time when I became brave enough to steal something. My mom had always taught me that it was wrong to steal, but my excuse was that I was hungry. I only wanted to take a little food from the Home Economics Class at school to help my growling stomach quiet down for the long bus ride home. I was scared but stole a chocolate candy bar. I smugly sat in the back of the bus and took a big bite. I quickly realized it was unsweetened and really bitter. I had enough respect for my bus driver not to spit it on the floor so I took my consequence and swallowed it. I learned a valuable life lesson that stealing isn't worth it.

That spring our family went to Cedarfield to visit Grandpa for Easter. I do not know how the fight between my parents began, but it was an enormous one this time. I did not even know it was happening, as I had spent the day with Holly just romping down by the river and being silly. When I arrived back at Grandpa's my mom was very upset and said that she and I were not returning to Heron Creek. She would register me in school at Cedarfield East right away.

Time to adapt again! Going from a school with fewer than 500 kids to a building with over 3000 was a shocker. I finished out the school year there. I don't know if I ever got used to the sheer size of the place, and just picking out a physical education class was a challenge. I went from girls P.E. to a counselor asking, "Okay, which of these twenty-two classes available would you like?" I was excited that I was able to get into a Driver's Education class there. This was actually a happy move, for me it meant I could go to school with Holly, be around Grandpa, and be out of the constant fighting at home.

I welcomed this change but did not like that it widened the gap between Brody and me. He chose to go back to Heron Creek and live with Dad. We each had to make a choice between our parents. It was a terrible position for any child to be put into.

Before the school year was completed my parents had made amends, and my mom went back to help with the resort. I stayed with Grandpa, choosing to spread my wings as a mixed-up teenager. During the next few months Holly's older siblings would keep us supplied with alcohol; we had a summer filled with fun, hangovers, and talks of love.

One day during August Holly handed me a small sheet of paper filled with text she said that her sister had given it to her and that I should read it. So I did. That night I recited the sinner's prayer. I confessed that I was a sinner and asked Jesus to come live in my heart. In that tiny upstairs room, I was sitting near the window at my grandpa's house. Even though the weather was hot and sticky I felt clean. I was consumed with a peace that I did not understand, but I deeply enjoyed. I knew something was different on the inside, but I did not know what to do or how to live my life any differently.

I was so disappointed at the end of the summer when my parents expected me to move back to Heron Creek to finish out high school there. I wish I could say that everything went well after that but I can't. I went deeper into the world of delusion by using alcohol and drugs so I could escape the pain. Things at home had not changed much and the atmosphere was still charged with friction and discord.

Not only was there turmoil in our home but even in our yard. Because our home was in the middle of the resort there was always a variety of people around. One evening I started to walk down the path to the lake, and an old gent came around the corner with a gun pointed at me. He had been a war veteran and thought I was the enemy. He started shouting at me to surrender or he would shoot. He must have been having some type of hallucination; it didn't take much talking to convince him I was not the enemy, but it sure terrified me.

I also entered a very unhealthy relationship with the brother of my first lover. The first guy had now totally rejected me and wasn't even speaking to me. It was a very odd way to begin a relationship. Their brother James, a friend and schoolmate of mine, was found dead in a ditch full of water. No one knows for sure but they think he had been drinking, lost control of the car, and went into the ditch. The water was too powerful for him to be able to get the door open, and he drowned.

At the funeral I told Torrey if there was anything I could do to help let me know. He took that as a cue to start a relationship with me, and he asked me out. He was generous with gifts, buying me a Fugi racing bike, a used car, and a big diamond ring. Of course I returned with some gifts of my own. He had a bad temper and broke his fist more than once while we were dating by hitting walls and other things. He never hit me. I was sure I had found happiness with someone who loved, accepted, and wanted to marry and take care of me forever. I knew we could live happily ever after.

I spent much of the last half of my senior year planning my wedding. Torrey and I went through marriage counseling at the Catholic church, spent every minute we could together. I worked as a nurse's aide at the local nursing home, and he worked at a local fast food joint and did some construction in a family business. The date was set for September, dress bought, announcements ordered, and everything was falling into place. I believed a peaceful happy life would soon be mine. How I did not get pregnant during this time was only by the grace of God. We chose not to use birth control since we were getting married and wanted many children anyway.

In the spring Torrey and I went out fishing on the Piper Flowage. We were out in a canoe making some small talk, and then he said, "I don't love you and don't want to marry you." I wanted to jump out of that boat or die on the spot; the rejection crushed me. I could only cry, I could not escape. I never saw it coming. I had him take me home and eventually gave him the ring back. I was devastated and just wanted to fall off the earth. My whole world had just come crashing down, all my plans, my dreams, and my hope for the future.

My mom was very supportive and just listened and let me cry, acknowledging the hurt I was going through. She helped me come up with a plan to look forward to. I would go live with her sister, my aunt Diane, who had moved to Illinois. Howie had passed away four years prior to this, and she was living alone. I had to just wait a few weeks until I graduated and turned eighteen.

Chapter 4

Three days after my eighteenth birthday I moved to Poplar, Illinois, so I could start a new life. Aunt Diane got me a job at the cord set factory in which she worked. I absolutely hated that job and admired her for working there for as long as she did. I guess she did not have much of a choice about going to work after her husband died, as he did not leave her with enough to live on. At the factory my job was to sit at a machine and cut the plastic that surrounded the wire on a cord so a plug could be attached. My hands were so blistered and sore I felt they would never heal, and my tail bone ached from sitting so long. I felt the bell system was inhumane and treated the workers like children.

I quickly looked for another job and got one working in a daycare just a short bike ride from the house. I liked working with the little ones much more than working at that factory. I really enjoyed riding my bike; I would sometimes ride my bike through the winding ritzy neighborhoods searching for a direction for my life and asking God if this is what life was like, moving along on unknown roads for unknown destination trusting Him to keep me safe. I didn't think He was listening or answering, but I kept searching and asking.

It didn't take me long to become romantically involved. Right across from the house where we lived was a wealthy Italian family with a son near my age. Aunt Diane introduced us. He was doing some carpentry work for her. He was trying to help her figure out why her roof had a small leak. As he spent a few days working on the roof we began to talk and get acquainted.

David was just a few years my senior and was very interesting. He had traveled the world and had just moved back from Hawaii. He helped me to learn about eating healthy. He was staying away from meat, preservatives, and eating a lot of fresh fruit and veggies. The main reason was because he was just getting over hepatitis from a dirty heroin needle. His main goal was to get healthy again.

We started going out eating at authentic Mexican and Chinese restaurants in and around the city. He taught me about exotic foods, we went hiking, swimming, sailing, gave each other massages, and had in depth conversations about life and love.

David was very responsible and made sure that we used birth control. He took me to a clinic in the city where I got a diaphragm to make sure I wouldn't get pregnant. The place was a huge building right in the heart of the city. I was glad he was comfortable taking me there, as it was very scary for me. The whole exam and fitting was very humiliating, as the man who examined me could not speak English and acted very angry.

David was clean from drugs and did not touch anything bad for his body at this point, but many of his friends were still into drugs. One day we met up with a bunch of people at a park for a big party. Some kind of pipe was being passed around, and many people were taking hits. When it came to me I tried a bit, but it instantly sent me into Neverland. The next thing I knew everyone was running in different directions because the authorities had shown up to break up the party. Good thing David was straight, or I might have been arrested or never made it home. He knew a back way through the woods to get me home safely. We later found out the stuff in the pipe had been laced with some chemicals.

I did a lot of reading and adjusting of my eating habits getting my weight down to an all-time low of one-hundred fifteen pounds on my five-foot-six-inch body. I felt good, and I was happy physically, but I also knew that something small was tugging at me spiritually. I did my best to ignore it.

Things were not going that great at the daycare, it was understaffed and short on budget. To earn some extra cash I did a some typing for David's dad, who was a lawyer.

I decided I wanted to try working in a nursing home again and found out there was one pretty close to the house. I applied and got hired right away. I liked this much better than working at the daycare. It was physically harder work, but I enjoyed the elderly people. One of the lovely older woman patients sticks out in my mind. She had escaped a concentration camp but still had the identifying tattoo on her wrist. Seeing that made the Holocaust more real to me and not just a story in a book. I have always appreciated older people and have been willing to care for them.

Near the end of the summer David decided to go spend some time on his property near Lake Superior. Things were a bit strained between Aunt Diane and me, as she did not approve of my eating or lifestyle, so when David offered to give me a ride back to Heron Creek I said, "Sure, I will go along." We packed all our belongings into his Ranchero and headed north.

Chapter 5

On the way the vehicle started acting up; David figured that the gas had all leaked out of the gas tank. We had to rig something up to keep the Ranchero running. We found a glass gallon bottle that once held orange juice and we bought some gas line. We made a miniature gas tank out of the jug, filled it with gas, and placed it on my lap in the front seat of the vehicle. At this point we realized that David could not drive the vehicle without me, I would have to hold gas line into the jug so that it wouldn't slip out. We had to stop often to fill the little tank.

On the way the mechanical problem was not our only trouble; we also had a flat tire. It was raining, and the tire was buried in the open back of the vehicle under all our belongings. That was quite a memorable and challenging trip. A part of me did not mind, as I was with someone who had accepted me.

We eventually made it to his aunt's house that was near his property. We tried to sleep that night out in the bucket-seat vehicle, not wanting to wake them up in the middle of the night, but it was too uncomfortable to rest.

The next morning after meeting his aunt we hiked out to the little silver trailer in the woods. There were two ways to get there: take an old overgrown logging trail, through a swamp, or cut through a horse pasture climbing under the barb wire fence to get in, crossing the field and then more barbed wire to get out. It was quite the hike.

We ended up staying there all of September, trying to get the vehicle fixed. We didn't know who to trust with the work and didn't have enough money to pay someone to do it. To stay busy we would go into town once a week where we took showers at the public sauna/bathhouse, and picked up a few groceries.

At some point I developed an uncomfortable urinary tract infection that was very painful. I was suffering miserably because I did not have any medical insurance and I couldn't afford to see a doctor. I ended up drinking lots of juice and water and was able to flush the infection out.

On one of our trips to town David talked me into trying to get some free food since we were running low on money and had no income coming in. I was very uncomfortable doing this but did not want to be rejected by him, so I went to Social Services to try to get food stamps. The authorities would not give me food stamps because I really did not have any proof of income. Social Services did give me a twenty-five-dollar certificate for groceries at the local store. We mostly lived on eggs and apples. We could pick wild apples on our hike to the trailer and eggs were cheap.

He must have borrowed some money from his aunt because one day we finally went to a garage so they could work on the vehicle. To our amazement we found out that the gas tank did not have a leak, and we never needed to hook it up the way we had. Did we ever laugh, knowing how much that gas problem had changed our plans and how, if it had not happened I probably would have had him drop me off in Heron Creek. I would have never seen Lake Superior nor spent the time together in Michigan.

When I finally called my mom and told her where I was living she asked if I would come for a visit. David had been invited to help in a sailboat race in Florida, and I wouldn't be able to go along.

I bought a Greyhound bus ticket and headed "home." It would have been a five-and-a-half-hour drive, but with all the layovers and bus switches it took over twenty-four hours. I met some very strange people on that bus ride. Good thing I had learned how to hold my own as a kid in the bars. The visit went okay and my mom told me that her aunt in Cedarfield really needed someone to take care of her because she was dying of cancer. I thought it would be nice to live in Cedarfield again, so I said I would do it.

First I had to drive back up to Michigan and get my belongings. My parents loaned me a car, and off I went. That was the longest driving trip I had ever taken by myself. Learning not to let fear hold me back I did it, even if I was a bit scared. I spent a few days and said goodbye to David, we left on good terms but never saw each other again. We did exchange a few letters and did talk on the phone a few times, but our lives went in separate directions.

My great-aunt Sylvia had been married to Grandpa's brother Rodger, but they had been divorced for quite a while. She needed assistance every day with meals, bathing, and housekeeping. She was dying of cancer and didn't know how much time she had to live. Since I had experience working in the nursing home I knew what to do to keep her comfortable, and I did not mind helping her. She paid me well, and I could leave at night and spend time with Holly or visit Grandpa.

A few weeks later my friend Jasmin from high school called me and asked if I wanted to work with her on a fancy dude ranch in Arizona. I was torn on what I should do, since my great-aunt continued to get sicker as the weeks passed; she was still alive, and I wanted to take care of her. I told Jasmin to send me an application, and if it went through it must be a sign that God wanted me to work there. Well, it did not take long for me to get the answer. I was hired as a waitress. Great-aunt Sylvia understood and was happy for me, yet in a way it was hard to leave. She died shortly after I moved away.

I was pretty excited to start a new adventure in my life. It was a bit frightening getting on that plane all by myself, but I was not about to let fear stop me from doing anything. I had flown a few times before, once to Georgia with Mom, Grandpa and Brody and also in a small ski-plane, but never alone.

Chapter 6

When I arrived in Phoenix I had to take a shuttle to the bus depot and then hop a Greyhound to Woolen Canyon. I was amazed at the surroundings, so many things that I had never seen before, it was a whole new world that I had only seen in books and on television. When I arrived in the bus depot a man named George with a huge port wine birth mark across his face picked me up and took me to Machado Ranch to see my new place and meet up with Jasmin.

I walked around in awe trying to take it all in. I took many photos, horses, cacti, sand, Joshua trees, and the mountains.

It was great to catch up with my friend Jasmin, whom I had not seen for several months. She showed me where I was going to live. My new living quarters were made out of cement blocks painted white. There were around ten different doors into the building that was "U" shaped. Between each door was a shared bathroom that would be used by four people. Jasmin and I shared a room with two twin beds. We shared our bathroom with two gals from Maine.

I had never waitressed before, and the ranch wanted it that way. They were very particular on everything. Our work clothes were provided. The calico skirt was exactly four inches above the knee, an apron, white blouse and white shoes completed the uniform.

The day after I arrived the training began. Outfits must be pressed, shoelaces snowy white, same with the apron, no stains or marks allowed. We had to learn how to carry the trays up on our shoulders. The first thing I lifted to my shoulder was two glasses of tomato juice, which briskly tipped over and spilled all down my back. It was embarrassing, but I learned quickly how to keep everything balanced.

We also learned in our training where each piece of silverware went and what direction it was placed on the table. I was taught how to put a coffee cup with the handle exactly at three o' clock, where the salad, soup and dessert was set, how to fold napkins, and what order things were served in. We worked three meals a day, six days a week. We were paid a good wage plus our room and board along with tips. We even received an end-of-the-year bonus if we stayed the whole season.

It didn't take long to meet everyone that worked there. There was a separate crew that worked in each area of the ranch: cooks, bakers, housekeeping, bar, office, dining room, barn, golf course, air strip, and grounds keepers. One or two people in each area got one day off a week. We quickly learned who had the same day off as we so we could do things together.

Since the clientèle who stayed there were usually rich and famous and were trying to get away from celebrity life and just be on vacation, we were told that we could not spend time with a guest when we were off duty, unless they asked us first.

The head gardener was happy to learn that he and I had the same day off and was quick to offer to take me sightseeing in his dune buggy. He was originally from New Jersey but had lived in Arizona quite a few years. We took many trips visiting old mines, desert dunes, dry riverbeds, canyons, Sedona, Prescott, and Flagstaff. We even arranged an overnight trip to California. We took the evening off before our day off and took the two co-workers from Maine with us. We were able to visit Disneyland, Knott's Berry Farm and the ocean. It was my first time to ever be that far West or to see an ocean.

Garrett became sweet on me and was always bringing me roses from the gardens. I wish I had thought about what I wanted in a man at that point in my life, but my self esteem was so low that anyone who brought me flowers, gave me gifts, and wanted to spend time with me and accepted me made me think I was "in love." Garrett was around ten years my senior. We became romantically involved. After a few months I realized that he had a heavy drinking problem. This really bothered me after what I had seen as a kid. I started getting on his case about his drinking, which only escalated the problem and put a wedge between us. That relationship ended, and I went into a depression, deeply feeling the rejection and believing I was unlovable or that something was wrong with me, and that no one wanted to love me.

Before Garrett and I had broken up we would frequently ride his motorcycle up in the mountains. Sometimes several other guys from the ranch would ride with us too. After the break-up I had a hard time filling up my day off. Sometimes I would go to the zoo in Phoenix, bike ride the few miles to town, go horseback riding, or just sit in my room and mope. My moods were highly dependent on where I was in my monthly cycle, too.

Jasmin tried to keep me busy with bus trips to the huge shopping mall and trips to the local bar. One of the times that sticks out in my mind was when she and I took the Greyhound to Phoenix and then hopped the city transit to the mall. We had a great day traversing through all the stores and spending all the money we had. In the evening when we returned to the bus depot we realized we had missed the last bus back to Wool Canyon. The bus schedules were changed because of daylight savings; we were unaware of this because Arizona does not change their clocks. We had to sit in a depot full of homeless people, pimps, and prostitutes until early into the morning. Trying to make the best of it we put our change together to try and buy a little food. We figured we had enough for an apple that we could split. As we were digging and counting we must have looked distressed, as a gal, obviously a prostitute, asked us if we needed change. We told her what had happened, and she gave us a few bucks for dinner.

One evening on my day off I was moping around the yard of our little complex, and Randy, the boyfriend of a co-worker, asked if I wanted to do something with him. I said, sure I had nothing planned. After he had a few beers he asked if I wanted to go for a ride on his motorcycle and I said, "Sounds fun! Do you think you could teach me how to drive one?" He was willing to do so.

I was feeling pretty immortal at the time, and I think the open-cockpit biplane ride I had recently taken gave me a little confidence that day. Maybe it was a death wish too.

Anyway, we hopped on the bike and he showed me how to shift. I got the hang of it, clutch, shift, faster and faster we went. I looked down at the speedometer that was over fifty-five miles per hour. As I looked up from checking the speed I saw a sharp curve coming at us really fast. I could not figure out how to get the bike to turn. The tire went off the blacktop and hit the gravel, the force of that knocked everything out of balance, sending us crashing to the ground. My eye slammed into the end of the handle bar before and on our way over the bike, and then Randy landed on top of me as I slid on the gravel, face first. I am not sure how far we slid, but I did pass out. Randy kept calling me and trying to wake me up. I couldn't open my eyes, but he said, "Get on the bike and hang onto me." He drove me back to the ranch.

My eye was completely swollen shut, everything hurt, and I had blood pouring out of my face, chest and arm. At the ranch Randy got me into Darin's car, and they rushed me to the hospital. Good thing Jasmin was available to come along; she filled out all the paper work for me. She even had to cup my hand like you do a child who is learning to write, then help me sign my name. I had to sign a document promising I would pay at least ten dollars a month to pay the hospital bill.

I did not have insurance, so I did not get any x-rays. I did get a thorough examination, checking for broken bones by moving each one. They cleaned the wounds and took some of the gravel out. The ambulance crew showed up at the hospital while I was there. Someone had called in the accident, and they were out looking for me. Once we told them where the crash happened they realized I was who they were looking for.

The doctor felt that I had no broken bones, the bleeding was under control, and I was coherent, so they released me. The crew made sure that Jasmin and I understood the directions on what I should or should not do after such a major concussion and with so much open skin.

I looked like something out of a horror movie. When one of the gal's I waitressed with saw me she vomited. A few hours later I was resting in my bedroom at the ranch when there was a knock at the door. I got up and opened it. A police officer was standing there. His mouth opened, and he gasped, "Oh, my God, you look like ground hamburger!" I did; from the top of my forehead right down to the top third of my chest. He then asked, "Were you driving the motorcycle? I replied, "Yes."

Next he asked, "Can I see your motorcycle license?"

I informed him that I did not have one.

He said, "I hate to do this, but it's my job." Then he proceeded to write me out a ticket. I had to pay a hefty fine for driving without a license. The first violation of my life.

Later I learned the motorcycle I crashed was totaled and never started again. It was a miracle that it even worked long enough to get me to the ranch. It was definitely a miracle that I survived the crash, since I did not have a helmet on.

It took several weeks for me to do much of anything. I could not work in the dining room with my face in such a mess, and I could not go outside or be in the sun, because of the concussion. I had to just sit around waiting for my wounds to heal and hope I would not lose my job and place to live. My co-workers could not stand to eat with me in the employee dining room, so Jasmin had to bring my meals to our room. It was terribly lonely. One gal did help wash my hair a few times, picking gravel out of my face and scalp as best she could. To this day there is still some embedded in my face. I also got a very bad infection where the scrapes were the deepest, over my right temple. When I was at a follow-up visit a very kind nurse slipped some expensive medicine into my pocket, as she knew I could not afford to buy it. There is a lifelong scar that daily reminds me of how God saved me from death that day, even if I did not acknowledge Him at that point in my life.

One fun benefit about working at such a ritzy place was all the people I got to meet who were famous. There were many that stayed at the ranch who were world-renowned, those in the political arena, entertainment business, and those who were wealthy. We were not allowed to know their last names unless they chose to tell us. Many were big tippers and very pleasant to serve, and of course a few were not. It really made me feel important and accepted when a famous rock star requested me as his waitress my second year there.

Trying to stay away from guys my age who just broke my heart and really wanting to get my act together and make something of my life, I got into a friendship with Bryce. He was a retired tennis pro. He lived off ranch but taught tennis part time there. He was old enough to be my father, and we decided we could adopt each other. We just enjoyed doing things together, like a father and daughter; there was no romantic involvement. If he had any in mind he never shared that with me. We would spend hours sharing about our lives, he always said that I had lived the life of a forty-year-old by age eighteen. He told me about the daughter that he knew existed, but he had not seen, and we filled a void for each other. We would go shopping, out to eat together, take walks, and go for drives.

One day he asked if I wanted to hike to the top of Buzzard Peak with him. I thought it would be great. We packed a picnic lunch and headed out there. He had climbed it several times before and wanted to take a more challenging way up. I was afraid of the tougher terrain and said I would take the easiest way up and meet him at the top.

I enjoyed the climb up to the top. Once we reunited we took in the view and had a nice lunch. He said he wanted to take the easier way down and I said I needed a bit of a challenge so I would take the harder way and meet him at the bottom. Off we set on different paths. When I reached the base I could not see him and figured if I just walked around the peak I could find his car.

After about an hour of searching and hollering I started to feel panic. There was no answer! I did not know what to do. I did remember that I could see the peak from the ranch and figured that maybe I could just hike to the ranch. I had to get back and go to work that night. I headed out, not thinking it would take me very long. I figured if I just got over a hill or two I would see the ranch, but as I mounted each point all I could see is another large desert hill to climb.

After several hours in the hot desert sun, I was thirsty, tired, and scared to death. I had run into several swarms of bees near cattle troughs and had huge blisters on my feet from my new tennis shoes that I had bought for the hike. I was pretty sure I was going to die that day.

I began apologizing to God for all the horrible things I had done in my life. I started to beg Him to let me live. I screamed, I cried, and I begged some more. Nothing. I was still alone. No one showed up to take me home. Then I started to bargain with God, promising I would live for Him if He would just let keep me alive and get me back safely.

It was getting dark and I figured I was going to get bit by a rattle snake, a scorpion or attacked by coyotes. I did not think God cared, so I just lay down on the sand to accept my impending death. I was cold and worn out and felt like I could not go on.

Lying there I could not get comfortable, so I got up and began to walk again, this time in complete darkness. I just couldn't give up like that. As I stumbled through the sand and cacti I noticed way off in the distance a tiny light. I headed toward the light even though pain ravished my whole body I had a glimmer of hope. As I continued toward the light I ran into a barbed-wire fence, I knew how to get through those from my time in Michigan! After I climbed through the fence I ran into moving water, some type of river or creek. I thought there might be quicksand, and now I would surely die. I continued to go forward and to my surprise the water was not very deep. I made my way all the way across getting very close to the light, I could now tell it was a street light in a trailer court.

After crossing the river I had to work my way through another barbed wire fence. I was in the trailer park! I went to the first house

I saw and knocked on the door. A little kid answered the door and started screaming, "MOM, MOM!" The lady quickly came. I explained my dilemma. She said she did not have enough gas in her car or the money to buy gas to take me to the ranch, but I could use her phone. I called for a ride.

I don't even remember who picked me up, but I did get scolded. A search party had been out for hours looking for me, I had missed my shift, and I was a mess. I felt so rejected for disappointing and bothering so many people. I just sunk my self in a tub full of cool water, cleaned up, and went to bed.

I had to work the next morning, sunburn, blisters and all. It didn't take me long to forget about my promise to God. Bryce told me that the owner of the ranch really chewed him out and told him he needed to stay away from me.

I was very prone to hormonal depression, feeling worthless and inferior pretty much every three weeks, as my cycle is only twenty-one days long. I was longing to figure out what direction I was supposed to go in with my life. Several times I allowed myself to get into relationships that were not healthy. With each one I went deeper into depression, hating my life and myself. I knew the ranch would be closing for the summer and had to come up with a plan for the next step in my life. Jasmin was going back to Minnesota, the last place on earth that I wanted to go. I had to find someplace else to live.

A couple that worked at the ranch in Arizona asked me and a few others from the crew if we wanted to work for them at a family-style dude ranch in Montana. I said sure and made plans to get there.

The season ended in May with a fun end of the year party around the pool. Everyone said their goodbyes. A handful of us got into Dorian's car and headed northwest, everyone with a different destination except one of the guys who washed dishes. He was going to Riverstone Ranch in Montana, too. Dorian offered to take Gordon and me as far as Casper.

On the way we stopped at a restaurant in Castle Green, since I was still a vegetarian I ordered a tuna salad sandwich. It did not take but an hour or so to realize I had food poisoning. Dorian was kind enough to drop us off at a motel in Cheriton, even though I was puking out of the car window the rest of the way.

Our plans had been to just hop a bus from that part of Wyoming to Montana, but I was too sick. I ended up in that motel for three days, wishing I could die. Surprisingly Gordon stayed with me. I am sure he thought I was going to die or end up in the hospital. With no insurance going to a doctor or hospital did not even seem like an option.

I thought Gordon was a real geeky guy and really kept him at a distance. I was grateful that he stuck it out with me for those three days, and would keep me company on the travels, but I did not want any kind of romantic relationship with him. He told me he wanted a deeper relationship with me. I refused and told him to put it out of his head.

We eventually made it to the bus depot, bought our tickets, and waited for our bus out of there. I received another lesson on homeless people. I could hardly believe my eyes as I watched people pull old sandwich crusts and cigarette butts out of the trash. Their destitution showed me a world of poverty that I had not seen before, yet somehow could empathize with.

Chapter 7

We arrived in Greenvale, Montana, after one o' clock in the morning. The bus dropped us off on the street because the depot was not open at this hour of the morning. We thought we could just walk to a motel and get a room. We started down the street, suitcases in hand. We did not even make it a block when a police officer stopped us. He asked for our identification and what we were doing at this time of morning. After we explained that we had jobs at the ranch he took us to a large home owned by a church group for a free place to stay.

An older gent, Howard, a retired professor from the college, gave us a lift the sixteen miles up the mountain to the ranch. There weren't very many workers there yet.

The living quarters looked like a house on the outside. It was divided into a guys' side and a girls' side with a living room in the middle. Inside the room had closets made into dividers to form twelve or sixteen little cubicles. Each cubicle had a bunk bed, built-in dresser, and closet. I was able to pick which one of the many in the girls cabin I wanted. I was the first girl to arrive, so I chose the one closest to the bathroom.

What a life encounter to get first-hand knowledge of this topography! I was in awe over the rocky mountains. I wasn't just viewing them from a distance, or looking at them in a book; I was right up on the top of a mountain. A more glorious splendor I never could have imagined. I could scarcely take it in.

I had so few belongings it didn't take me long to get unpacked and start exploring my new surroundings. A river ran through the place and mountain peaks were everywhere that I looked.

I also had to find the boss and learn what my responsibilities would be. I learned that I only had to serve breakfast and supper, as the guests were on their own for lunch. I did have to take a turn at cleaning cabins, something I had experience in from my teen years at the resort. This small ranch in the mountains had a little variety store, recreation room for the guests, many cabins, and a small restaurant. There was a herd of horses and some mules I could ride whenever I wanted to. I knew from the beauty of this place it was where I was supposed to be, even if it did snow that first week of May.

It didn't take long to meet the staff there, as this ranch was much smaller than the one in Arizona. There was Cal who ran the barn and led mule trips into the wilderness, his wife Susie who headed up housekeeping. The couple that had invited me to work there arrived soon. She ran the dining room and he the kitchen. A couple local guys helped in the kitchen, and a few others helped with grounds keeping and cabin upkeep. Within a couple weeks more gals showed up who would work the dining room with me. A couple of them I had worked with in Arizona.

I tried to be nice to everyone, yet I seemed to have a hard time communicating with the gals. I just did not get into catty discussions about hair, nails and fashions. I preferred to be out in the woods or hang with the guys who I thought I understood. Of course this alienated me from the girls even more.

I tried to focus on my work, doing the best I could and spending the rest of my time taking in the beauty that surrounded me. I would ride the horses on craggy mountain trails along cliffs every chance I got. I was glad to have my bike around, too, so I could either ride farther up the mountain, or take the sixteen-mile ride down the mountain. I learned that you can be heading down the mountain but still have to pedal up hill when riding on a bike.

I really don't know why I didn't get along with the other girls better. I am sure my feelings of worthlessness and having no value in myself caused me to just feel used and abused. Some of the girls would help themselves to my things without asking. Maybe since I never had a sister I could not understand, but I just thought it was rude. I bought a locking trunk so they would not use my iron or take any of my personal belongings without permission.

Sometimes I would join them at parties after work, but once I got there I would feel so left out in the crowd I would leave crying. I am sure that my hormonal patterns also played big into this. One night I was so hurt at a party that although we were many miles from the ranch I up and left. I started hiking along the highway in the dark of night. I became scared and wondered if I would run into some wild animal, yet the fear was not as big as the hurt and rejection, so I kept on walking. It was not very long before a car came along. I stuck out my thumb and was offered a ride by a very nice man. I am not sure why I was brave enough to hitchhike.

That night was not the first time I had hitchhiked. I had thumbed a ride a handful of times so I could get to or from town. I figured I was safe because I was so near a college town and the ski area of Rocky Butte where many teens hitchhiked. Maybe it was just a death wish too; my self esteem hit an all-time low and most days I really did not care if I lived or died.

In the depression I spent a lot of time alone with no purpose in life. I gained a lot of weight trying to drown my sorrows with food. I just wanted a place to belong and feel loved and accepted.

One thing that made me very happy was that Holly and her friend Brina took a Greyhound bus from Minnesota to come out to visit me for a week. We went white-water rafting and horseback riding and enjoyed sharing many hours together.

I spent much of my free time hanging out with the guys. One of them started really sharing a lot about his life with me. Chad had been divorced and had just walked out of a relationship in Hawaii. He thought some time apart might strengthen their bond. He was not looking for a new relationship but was missing intimacy. I said I felt the same and would be willing to be intimate without all the trappings of commitment to fill my lustful desires, or whatever an eighteen-year-old calls her sexual drive. It seemed to work for both of us for a while. Since he worked maintenance he had keys and access to every place on the ranch. He created a little nook in the attic above the laundry room for us to escape off to without anyone else knowing where we were.

My nineteenth birthday just happened to be on my day off. Since this ranch was so much smaller no one else had the same day off as me. I was all alone and had no one around to share it with me.

My mom had sent a big package for my birthday full of collector gnomes and other surprises. The head cook, who was quite a portly man, picked up the mail for me that day. I could not always take the time it took to travel the six miles round trip to the post office by bike. When he gave me my package he was very mad at me. He explained it to me, and I realized his embarrassment. The tape came loose on the package, and it had popped open in the post office, spilling all the packing out on the floor. As he picked up all the "packing peanuts" he realized that they were tampons. My mom, being thrifty and practical, used them as packing material, since she could get them for quite a deal from a nearby paper mill, and she knew I could use them. He vowed never to pick up my mail for me again.

Feeling sorry for myself on my birthday I decided to just go on a long bike ride and wallow in my pity party. I packed a small lunch and headed up the mountain. I knew there was reservoir up top and a grandiose view. I had been up there a few times. When a number of us would want something to do after work we would pile into someone's car and go up there. It was exciting to listen to the mountain goats ram heads together. I had never heard such a forceful echoing sound before.

This particular day had a few extra obstacles. Part way up the mountain I came up on a herd of long horned steer. They were being herded up the mountain to greener pasture. I thought about turning around, but decided I had nothing better to do, and I did not think the herd could be very big. Wow, was I wrong. I had to swerve around cows and calves almost the entire way up to the top, it was quite an experience. Once at the top I took a rest and then had to ride down, going through the crowded road dodging mooing mother cows and calves, knowing those long horns could gorge me to death.

The staff at the ranch had a Christmas party on June twenty-fifth. It was nice to find out that a couple of the girls thought I was okay, as they gave me small gifts. One of the gals was from Colorado and really liked to camp. As we talked about it we decided it would be great if we could go on a one night camping trip. I didn't have much for goals in my life at this time, but something I really wanted to do was camp out in the wilderness. We picked a date, and two other gals decided to join us. I bought a sleeping bag, one gal already had a tent, and we were good to go. We had a great time even though we had to be back to work the next day.

The Fourth of July is just a few weeks after my birthday, and it fell on my day off, too. I was able to go to Rocky Butte for the parade. It was just a small local parade, where the townsfolk walked the few blocks through the downtown area. When they reached the end the whole parade started to march backwards, reversing the path they had just taken, but they still were facing forward, as they walked backwards. It was hilarious.

I was able to go into Greenvale for the celebrations that night. It was the first time in my life that I had seen a fireworks light show. I really could not remember seeing any fireworks as a child. The year before David had brought me to a golf course where we could see several different Chicago suburbs fireworks from a distance. I was astonished at all that I saw in that small college town settled in the mountains.

Something else I did that summer in Rocky Butte was seeing a triple X movie at the theater. I had never seen one before, and it gave the group of guys I went with something to talk about for quite some time. It also gave Chad an idea that he did not share with me right away. He waited until one night when a bunch of us had downed a few drinks. He decided it would be fun to sneak into the recreation room. He said since he had a key we weren't really breaking and entering. even though we were; my sense of judgment was not good because of the alcohol.

We were creeping around the store, being careful not to make noise or turn any lights on. The guys even helped themselves to a few items. I would not take anything. I had learned my lesson about stealing in high school and dared not take a thing. We had carried some alcohol along with us and had a few more drinks. Next we went into the recreation room to play a few games of pool. Before I knew it Chad started kissing me and forced me down on a rug. He wanted sex right then and there. I was too drunk to fight him off. I closed my eyes, hoping it would be over soon, but then all of a sudden the other two guys joined in, with all three guys raping me. I was too stunned to say anything, too afraid to scream knowing we would get caught inside the place we were not supposed to be.

The next day I informed Chad I would never sleep with him again, and I didn't. This whole incident haunted me and increased my feelings of worthlessness and inadequacy. I felt guilty, blameworthy for this wrongdoing because I let myself become vulnerable. I chose to not share what happened with anybody.

I found it very difficult to sleep for several reasons. The main one being, I am a light sleeper. With so many girls sleeping in one place the room was never quiet. When I could not sleep I would slip out of the room and go to the middle room to watch television. There was not much on at that time of the morning but a show captured my attention. A man was talking about world news and how it lined up with what the Bible said. I started listening to this television preacher, he talked about the love of Jesus and asked me to pray with him. I said the prayer with him being highly aware that I was sinner. But then something else happened inside that reminded me of the day I prayed at Grandpa's house. I could not figure out how to carry that "good feeling" with me after the program was over. It reminded me of the shows Mike's mom used to listen to when I was in High School. The man talked about a personal relationship with Christ as if Jesus was not just someone in history but a friend that could be talked to all the time. My concept of God, Christ, and the Holy Spirit was very unclear, but it did make me think about that promise I had made to God to "serve" Him, if he let me live and get out of the desert. God had held up His end of the bargain, but I was very aware that I had not. I called the eight-hundred number and asked for a free Bible.

September was the end of the season at the ranch. It came none too soon for me. I was ready for a change, but once again I was faced with the question what was I to do with my life. I decided my best option was to go back to the ranch in Arizona for another season.

First I wanted to go to Minnesota to visit. I especially wanted to see my mom, grandpa and Holly. I also wanted to talk Holly into moving to Arizona with me.

I bought a one-way train ticket to Minnesota. My mom was faithful to pick me up at the depot. She still lived in Heron Creek, but we stayed in Cedarfield for the visit. Mom's sister Darla, her husband Henry, and a couple of my cousins were there. I really enjoyed seeing Grandpa and Holly again. I did not have to twist Holly's arm very hard; she was willing to go West with me. She sent in her application. She was hired. We bought our plane tickets and headed to Wool Canyon.

Chapter 8

It was fun showing Holly around the ranch, meeting up with old friends and getting to know a whole bunch of new crew members. The ranch had built some new staff rooms that were much nicer. We had a private bathroom, big closet, paneled walls, and carpet. Holly and I shared a room.

She was hired to work in housekeeping and before you knew it we were into a routine of working and living together.

It wasn't long before I found out that Sam, one of the new busboys from Maine, was sweet on me. I still wanted to be accepted and wanted to find "true love," so it didn't take very long before we were spending time together. He enjoyed running and had even done the Boston Marathon. Many days when he ran he would invite me to come along. I was not a runner, so I would ride my bike alongside him. We really developed a good friendship, doing many healthy things together. Ideas of marriage were playing in the back of my mind, and we even talked of that possibility together. We became intimate, and sex became a big part of our relationship way too soon. Sam was a great listener and truly felt sorry for me when I shared how hard my life had been. I continued with my monthly premenstrual crying jags. He would always try to comfort me through them. Even though the attention made me feel accepted it also fed the pity party, making me more miserable.

Very few of the workers at the ranch had a vehicle, and as much as I liked to ride my bike I was tired of doing it all the time. I did not want to bum rides, take buses, or hitchhike anymore. I wanted independence and to be able to see my surroundings and own my own car. I went to a local car dealership and inquired about purchasing a car. The guy was very gruff and wanted to know if I wanted new or used. I told him I was unsure and he told me to come back when I was sure. This just irritated me enough to cause me to go to the other dealership in town.

At the other garage the guy treated me with respect and had me take a Bobcat out for a spin. I really liked it and thought it would be great. He helped me start the paperwork, and made sure I was approved for a loan. I was so excited I could hardly contain myself. The salesman, playing on my youth and naivety, told me that he had an even better deal for me, a car that was pretty much the same thing, only it was white and the price was less. The total cost would be under five thousand dollars. I jumped at that since I was very penny-wise with my money.

First I had to get the insurance, license, and loan papers all set up and signed. Once we did that I asked for a tank of gas, thinking I was being pretty studious with my money. He wrote me out a voucher for gas and then handed me the keys, walking me to my brand-new Pinto Pony. I sat in it, put the key in the ignition and realized it was a stick shift. I had no clue how to drive it. I felt very foolish, but he was a good sport called his son in to give me a lesson. I learned pretty quickly, and off I went clutching, shifting and enjoying my new-found freedom.

Sam was happy that I had a car ;we were able to make many trips in it. Our favorite destination was Phoenix. We went to the state fair several times and some sporting events. One night we were leaving a game, I don't recall which sport it was. As we pulled out of the parking lot on to a six-lane road I realized that I had pulled into the lane where another car already was. We collided. There was the sound of metal crunching before I could even react. The driver's side front end was totally smashed in. No one was hurt, but everyone was very shook up. The other car was totaled. The police arrived right away, and I received a ticket for "failing to yield," my second citation since moving to Arizona. My car was drivable, but I was too upset to drive. I insisted that Sam drive. He had to learn how to drive a stick shift that night. Insurance covered the damage, and it was fixed good as new within a short time.

Holly and I would take trips to the mall or over to Yuma. We even found a place not to far away where there was a life size replica of Jesus's tomb that we both liked to spend time at. We both wanted something more spiritually; we wanted to know what truth was, but we were at a loss as to how to find out. We did attend mass in town once in a while, but we were not finding what we were seeking.

I often times felt torn between spending time with Holly or spending time with Sam. I tried to do things with both but eventually took my friendship with Holly for granted and looked to Sam for love and acceptance.

Sometime after Christmas Holly and I decided we wanted to go to Mexico. We started planning and making arrangements to get a little time off from work. We located maps and decided where we wanted to go and how we would get there. Sam said he wanted to go along, and a gal who worked in housekeeping with Holly desired to go, too.

After making all the arrangements necessary the four of us took off for Tucson in my car. We did not get on the road until late at night. We drove to a home that was owned by friends of Ellie's and slept the night there. In the morning we toured a dude ranch, visited an art gallery, a mission, a museum, and of course Mexico, eating at "The Cove." It was a very fascinating voyage.

Not long after we returned to work from our trip Sam started getting distant with me. I could feel the rejection, and as despair starting to set in I reacted with the fight defense. I confronted him, begging him to tell me what was wrong. Fear just gripped me as he finally let me know he had eyes for Ellie. Here was more proof that I was unlovable and that nobody wanted me. On the trip he had learned that Ellie was a Christian, and since he was one also he felt she would be better for him. I was so heartbroken over another rejection that I felt useless. I knew that I still had to work with him for several more months I was unsure if I could even do that. I needed a plan and direction for my life but where could I go?

Somehow I came up with the idea of joining the service. I figured that would head me into a positive direction. I tried to talk Holly into entering the Air Force with me. She was not convinced it was a good idea for her but she supported me. I started the process. I did great on the written tests and passed the physical.

The lady recruiter tried to get me to see I was much brighter than I thought I was since I scored so well on the test. My self esteem was too low to accept that I had a brain with any capabilities to use it. I did feel settled that I finally had some kind of future plan, a direction that might actually help me make something of my life. I was excited to hear that I would get to move to Texas for basic training and then move on where I would eventually get a job in electronics. The great part was that the Air Force would train me in every aspect and pay for it. I would get to travel and have all my room and board taken care of also.

I was still down about Sam but glad that I was able to get in the delayed-enlistment program. I just needed to stay busy until the fall, and then I would be on my way to San Antonio with a fresh start on life. The recruiter checked on me often and would take me to the base whenever she could.

Into the picture steps a new bus boy, Rick. He was from Indiana and had just moved to Wool Canyon. He had dropped out of college and had moved in with one of his brothers who was teaching in town at the middle school. Rick got a job at the ranch working in the dining room. I was not interested in him in the least. I had reached a point that I did not want my heart broken by any man ever again; I had a direction, and I had a plan, and I did not want to open myself up for any rejection.

Maybe Rick took this as a challenge, because he tried everything to get me to go out on a date with him. I kept trying to blow him off but he persisted, bringing me flowers and paying a lot of attention to me. I finally agreed to one date, planning not to have a second date and hoping that he would then leave me alone. Well he was such a gentleman on the date I succumbed to going on another date. Before long we were intimately involved, something I was not ready for again.

Since Holly was my roommate, and he lived with his brother we had a very hard time finding private time together. So two teens in lust will come up with a plan. We found our own place to rent, and I moved off the ranch, leaving Holly, reasoning that she would be going back to Minnesota soon, because the Ranch was closing for the season.

Rick knew that I was fully intending on going into the Air Force in the fall. We had a great time setting up the house, having friends over, and having parties whenever we could. The two of us had to make some decisions about what we would do for the summer. Our options were wide open, which made it even harder to figure out what to do or which way to go. Eventually we decided we would go by one of his brothers in Utah. His brother said there would be work for Rick and me both there.

Chapter 9

Before setting out on the journey we did a weekend in Las Vegas. We had a good time, enjoying the Hoover Dam and Four Corners along the way. We spent most of our time at the Black Jack machines. At one point I went to a window to cash in a Travelers Check. The attendant refused to cash it because I was under twenty-one. It was ironic that I had never been carded or asked for any type of identification while gambling but when doing something perfectly legal I was refused.

We finally set out on our long journey to Utah. His brother, who lived with a girlfriend, let us stay at their house until we could find a place to stay. We eventually found a place we could afford. It was a condo right in Winnie Falls. It was on the third floor and had a view of the mountains and ski hills that was spectacular.

Rick was able to get into construction work with his brother. I got a job at a nearby daycare. I enjoyed the kids, but after a while I did not like the lady in charge. One of my weekly duties was to do the shopping for the daycare. She would give me a list of the exact items, size and brand she wanted. I would use my car and go to the only grocery store around and get exactly what she had on the list, nothing more, nothing less. Every time I brought the items in she would go ballistic over the price. I took her anger personally, and instead of dealing with it I quit.

I needed to get another job, so every week I stopped at a motel restaurant asking if they would hire me to waitress. I'm not sure if they hired me because they needed help or they got tired of me bothering them. I really enjoyed waitressing again and made good money and some really nice friends. My favorite was Molly, a lady in her sixties, who was just getting by. Her husband was sickly, and they did not have any insurance. She and I could run that whole dining room by ourselves and make some really great tips doing it. We would really help each other out, putting the toast in for each other or giving coffee to one another's customers. When the manager added a third waitress on the shift, it was like tossing a wrench into an engine. Everything would get messed up, toast burned, tables missed, and unhappy customers..

Rick and I got out quite a bit since there were an abundant number of select places to hang out at. The community was geared to people our age. We could play backgammon, have dinner, or just sit and drink at these places.

I had my impending entrance to the Air Force hanging over my head, something I was not wanting to be committed to anymore. I tried to forget about it as much as possible.

On my twentieth birthday a group of people from Rick's work got together with us to help me celebrate. We hit a local Mexican Restaurant that was having a Margarita night. We had a really nice time. It felt good to be with people who had accepted me and wanted to be with us.

A few weeks after my birthday we were at a party at Rick's brother's place, where there was a bunch of drinking, coke snorting, and hash and marijuana smoking going on. Rick did not do drugs and discouraged me from doing any either. I had never snorted coke and was actually afraid of it, so I decided a lesser evil did not look so bad. I had smoked that in the past, so why not take a few hits of hash? I had not done any drugs since that episode in Chicago. I did not like the feeling and started getting paranoid.

Within a couple days I was in so much abdominal pain I wanted to die. I had no idea what was wrong with me. Fearing hospital bills and a ride in an ambulance I drove myself to the hospital. They took me and started tests. One possibility was a tubal pregnancy, another was a severe infection.

The urine test came out negative; I was not pregnant. The doctor put me on heavy-duty antibiotics and pain pills then told me to go home.

I was in miserable pain. I could not go to work, eat, or do anything but sleep and moan.

The following day I received a call from the hospital. My blood test came back positive. I was pregnant. I denied the possibility; immediately I thought it would be impossible, I always used a diaphragm. I was careful and had other plans for my life. This just could not be. The lady who called said I had to come in for a full exam. The rush of emotions mixed with the pain pills was more than I could handle. I cried, I writhed in pain both physically and emotionally. What was going to happen with my life? Was I ready for a baby? What would my parents think? What did the drugs and alcohol do?

Rick tried to make it into a positive and said that at least I could use this situation to get me out of my Air Force commitment.

The next week I went in and had an ultrasound. I was definitely pregnant. The man doing the ultrasound said it must have started attaching to my tubes but then moved. It was no longer an ectopic pregnancy, which would have explained the pain. I have been told it is impossible for an attached fetus to move, so I really do not understand what happened medically. I do know the pain had subsided.

Next I was told by either the doctor or nurse to make an appointment in a few weeks. When I was farther along they could take care of everything. It would cost about three-hundred dollars. I went back to work and tried not to think about the whole situation, but I could not think of anything else. I did share with a few of the other waitresses, and two confided in me that they had had abortions and that there was not much to it.

Rick agreed it was the best choice. He helped come up with the money and promised that he would stay with me if I got rid of the fetus. We could plan to have a nice future together. I was going to get a medical discharge from the Air force, and we both had good jobs. I let my recruiter know so she could get me all the paper work necessary for a medical discharge.

I continued to waitress, but was in mental anguish over the whole situation. The idea of having a baby who would love me was growing, yet still unseen. The idea of staying together with Rick, who seemed to have accepted me, was a hard choice to give up.

The day arrived for the procedure, first I had to sit with a counselor who gave me all the information I needed about the procedure. They would gently insert a small salt stick, smaller than a tampon. I would then go back to work for a few hours; when I returned they would take a small vacuum that would remove the embryo. She made it sound so simple and easy. Just like that my life would be fixed, all my problems would just disappear into a vacuum.

From deep within me came a grief that started to grow larger with each passing second. I began to weep as the whole thing was described to me. I knew from my inner core this was not right. The next thing I knew, I was being ushered into a sterile procedure room, and given a paper gown. I took off all my clothes and put the paper gown on, and I climbed up on the table to wait for the doctor.

The longer I lay there the more intense the sobs became. By the time the doctor came into the room I had reached hysteria. He pulled out the stirrups and told me to place my feet in them. My legs were trembling. My weeping was so out of control he told me to sit up. He looked me right in the eye and said, "Do you want this procedure, or not?"

I very sheepishly said, " I don't know."

He told me to get dressed, get my money back, go visit my family, and take more time for making this decision. I had a long time before I had to make up my mind, actually several more months in which it could be done.

First I had to tell Rick that I did not do what he wanted. I was filled with trepidation knowing he would reject me. I hated to do anything that I knew would cause conflict and possible rejection but the desire to keep my baby was stronger than the urge to avoid conflict.

Now I had to call my parents and tell them what was going on. They said it would be fine for me to come home for a visit. I bought a round trip ticket to Minnesota.

A few days later Rick drove me to the airport. I sojourned alone once again. My mom drove from Heron Creek and met me in Minneapolis.

Chapter 10

Our time together went well. The visit was only for one week. We cried, we talked and we made amends. At that point I had not totally made up my mind what to do. I was unsure if I was ready to become a single mother. I really wanted to hear Rick say that he had changed his mind and would marry me and help me raise this baby. I wanted him to accept me and our baby.

I journeyed back to Utah, knowing I had to talk it over with Rick one more time. I had decided if he would not change his mind I would return to my parents' home. He met me at the airport with my car. We headed to our place in Winnie Falls. As we were traveling a huge snowstorm moved in. We did not have enough money to get a hotel. The authorities stopped us at a tunnel, they wanted all vehicles to have chains on the tires. Since we did not have chains for my Pinto Pony, I did not think they would let us through, but they did. Rick tried his best to push through the storm and keep the car on the road. Eventually he lost control and slid into the ditch. We crawled out of the car, pulled my suitcase out of the back, and started to hitchhike through the dark and pelting snow. It wasn't too long before someone stopped to give us a ride. I was glad to get a lift even if it was from a stranger. My suitcase was heavy, and Rick refused to help me with it. I was also starting to feel the effects of my pregnancy, feeling sick to my stomach quite often.

The next few days I cried repeatedly. Rick made it perfectly clear that I had to choose him or the baby; I could not have both. I made my decision.

I called my parents and told them I had made up my mind, and I was moving back to Minnesota. My dad said he would catch the first plane he could get and would meet me at the airport, and he would drive me back home. The journey took a few days but went well. It was a good time for my dad and me to get to know each other on an adult level and let go of some old grudges. I felt he really had sympathy for me and wanted me back.

Chapter 11

The taverns became a headache for my parents. Trying to run them from so many miles away was tough. It was hard to find managers that were trustworthy. They finally decided to just sell the one out at the lake and keep the one in town.

While I was living out West my parents had bought an old house ten miles out of Heron Creek. They spent a great amount of time fixing it up. The plan was to move in before the baby was born.

It was exciting to see all the changes that had happened at the resort, too. Dad had remodeled all the cabins, and now only had housekeeping cottages. Since there were no overnight cottages the work load there changed. Mom was able to work at the local grocery store. Everything was not perfectly peaceful and nice, my parents still had disagreements, but my mom had reached a point where she would not argue anymore.

Dad was still driving truck for the potato farm. There were people in and out of our house often, especially drivers from the farm. I met most of them, but the one I got to know the best was a man called Ivan. He shared the eighteen-wheeler semi with Dad. He was going through a divorce and was having a rough time with it. He and his wife were getting along sometimes and were trying to divorce without to many complications. She would come over to our house once in a while when she went along with Ivan on hauls, or she would come over to pick him up when he was done working. My parents always invited them in for something to eat or drink.

That winter my mom put on a really nice baby shower for me. Even Ivan's wife, who had become his ex-spouse by then was there.

I had to find a doctor and get some help with medical bills. I was unaware of all the government programs out there. I ended up at Social Services and found out I qualified for Medical Assistance, WIC (Woman, Infant and Children government food supplement) and AFDC (Aid for Dependent Children). I wanted to help with finances, so I started selling Avon door to door to earn a little cash.

I enjoyed a closer relationship with my brother Brody, who was a senior in high school. We spent a great deal of time together getting to know each other better.

The pregnancy was pretty normal but I did have a few complications. One time mom and I traveled to Cedarfield to see Grandpa, and when we got there I had blood in my urine. After many tests and no conclusions the best solution the doctors could offer was that I sat too long in the car.

At Christmas time I was shopping downtown Heron Creek. It was snowing very hard. When I went to step toward the car I slipped off the curb, hurting my ankle. My mom rushed me to the hospital, where I had x-rays and found out it was sprained. I knew I had done real damage to it when I was hiking in the mountains with Rick in the summer but not being able to afford medical help I had just wrapped it up and walked on it. I had to use crutches for six weeks.

I gained twenty-five pounds and stayed pretty small, so they did do an ultrasound to make sure everything was fine. It all looked good. My mom attended birthing classes with me so she could be my coach. Things at home seemed more settled than I had ever remembered them.

I had a very odd and frightening incident happen while I was pregnant. In this situation a tenant who was renting a cottage from my parents was very upset. I was just walking out in the back yard when I heard her start to scream, "I'm going to kill you!" Then I saw what she was so stirred up about.

Duke, my brother's Irish Setter, had jumped her female dog, who was in heat. They were stuck together. We tried dumping cold water on them, but they remained connected. The woman was getting more and more hysterical. She decided the only solution was to kill Duke. She ran into the cabin and grabbed a pistol. She loaded it and aimed it at the dog, planning on finishing him off right there. I began shouting and crying, begging her not to kill him. I tried to reason with her that she might even shoot her dog by accident. I was afraid she was going to shoot me, but I got between her and dogs. When the dogs separated she eventually calmed down. All the emotion and then realizing that it was possible for my baby and me to have been killed was too much; I just collapsed.

Chapter 12

I was happy to learn my friend Mike was still in the area. I gave him a call and updated him on my life. He asked if I wanted to get together. We spent some time together either going to a movie, out to dinner, or just hanging out at his mom's house. It was nice to know he did not reject me and would still be my friend.

One day Mike's sister invited us to her church. She attended an Assembly of God church. They were having a guest speaker, and she thought we might get something out of it. I don't remember a word that preacher said, but I do remember feeling a peace I had never felt before. There was something here; maybe that truth that I was searching for, definitely a love that was tangible. That evening I noticed blue haze filled the room. I really did not give it much thought since I assumed it was incense. Later I found out they did not burn incense there and that it was the Shekinah Glory of God.

On the first Friday of May the labor pains began. My mom and I timed them and decided it was time to head to the hospital. It was around ten that night that we checked in. A nurse examined my cervix and hooked me up to an intravenous machine. As time passed and the contractions became less intense. I was advised to walk around as much as possible. My mom assisted me on each step, helping me drag the IV machine along. Every crack in the tile, piece of artwork on the wall and window in the building became familiar to us.

On one of the rounds through the waiting room we struck up a conversation with a couple there. She was obviously very pregnant too. They were waiting to see the same doctor that I had. Excited and a bit nervous they were having their first baby also. She was positive that she was in labor. Since, they lived in a little town nearly forty miles away they wanted to get to the hospital as soon as possible. We ended up talking quite a few times that night as Mom and I continued walking and circling around to the waiting room every lap.

The couple was eventually sent home when they found out she was in false labor. Mom and I continued to walk through the night, the contractions came about every ten minutes. They were mild enough that I could continue to walk through most of them, just pausing to brace myself for a minute or two once in a while.

The two of us continued to walk all of Saturday and Sunday, still no baby. Just fatigue. I refused to take any kind of pain pills, not even an aspirin, as I did not want any drugs in my baby's system. There was talk of doing a C-section, but the doctor decided to wait until Monday.

Bright and early Monday morning the nurses wheeled me down to the emergency room on a Gurney. The doctor broke my water with an amniotic hook, and the intense labor began. I started to scream with each contraction. I could not remember experiencing such excruciating pain ever before. The fatigue added to the discomfort. The baby was staying on one side, facing nose up. I was in such pain the medical staff continued to stress that I needed to take something to ease the pain. I stubbornly refused, not wanting to let anyone know the fear I had that my baby could have problems from drugs I had used during the first trimester. I wanted no drugs in my baby. I wanted to have everything as natural as possible.

The nurses demanded that I stop screaming. They taught me how to breathe properly and how to concentrate on my focal point. It did help me not to moan and scream so loudly. The baby heart monitor was showing signs that the baby was in distress, so I had to lie on my right side the rest of the day. Everything was so intense and lasted so long, I did not think I could do it. Finally at 5:00 p.m. on the dot my baby boy was born.

My perineum was ripped and cut in several places. I needed many stitches. I had several names in mind but had settled on Jonathon when

I found out it meant, "God is gracious." He was turning blue and had
a very low APGAR score. His brain was swelling from the traumatic
delivery, and he had large cut across his face from the amniotic hook.
The obstetric staff let me hold him for a minute and then whisked him
off to give him oxygen and a full exam.

At midnight his lung collapsed; they asked me permission to give
him a spinal tap. I was afraid he was not going to make it. There was
nothing I could do. I was exhausted and attached to too many tubes.
I could just sleep and whimper. He became jaundiced.

The first time the nurses had me stand up to try walking I passed
out and almost fell on the floor. It was painful to walk or move. I was
swollen so much that I could not void and had to have a catheter
inserted so my bladder could empty.

Jonathon was getting better quickly, but I was getting worse. The
medical staff determined that I had a urinary tract infection. Each day
the catheter would be removed, and I would try to void. I could not,
so I had to go through the pain of having another catheter inserted. It
took several days before I could urinate on my own. I was not allowed
to leave the hospital until I did. It was in for over a week.

When I finally was able to go home the infection came with me.
It just wouldn't go away. Oral antibiotics were not clearing it up, so the
doctor decided I needed to get antibiotics injected. I had to go into the
hospital every eight hours for several days. Just before I was heading
over to the hospital for my next injection I noticed a wood tick stuck
into Jonathon's back. I had the nurse in the emergency room pull the
tick out of Jonathon's back. The whole episode was very emotional
for me. I already had seeds of doubt if I was capable of being a good
mother.

The antibiotic was not strong enough to knock out the infection that
was spreading throughout my body, and causing a fever, aches pains.
I was filled with fear. The doctor decided I needed to be back in the
hospital on intravenous antibiotics. It devastated me that Jonathon
could not come back into the hospital with me. He had to stay with my
mother, but she did sneak him in for visits as much as she could.

The couple Mom and I had met earlier were back at the hospital. This time it was the real thing, and they had a baby girl. I was able to walk around with the IV bottle on wheels, so I wandered down to the maternity ward to peek at the new baby. The new mom saw me looking through the window and invited me to hold her baby. I told her my whole story and held that little girl for over an hour. I wanted to stay in contact so we exchanged phone numbers and addresses. I don't even remember how much longer I was in the hospital, but I was sure happy to go home and be with my beloved Jonathon; none of the pain and trauma compared to the love I had for him.

By June I was feeling much better. I wanted to get off of state aid so I turned to the job I knew best, waitressing. I did cocktail only at one and meals at the other. Mom watched Jonathon while I worked, but I brought him along when I went door to door selling Avon.

I had Jonathon baptized at Catholic Church in Otter Bay. I asked Brody to be Jonathon's godfather and Holly to be his godmother. The priest had forgotten about the baptism, so at the end of the service he had just the family come up. Holly brought her fiancé Warren along for me to meet. The priest ended up having Brody stand in the position of father and Warren as godfather. The whole thing was strange, but at least I was sure I was starting my baby off on a spiritual path.

Brody graduated from high school that spring; then he decided to join the Navy. Sometime that summer he headed to California for boot camp. My mom confided in me that she was moving out for good now that Brody had left; she had only stayed for our sakes. Mom packed a few things and left for Cedarfield to live with her dad.

I did not want to leave my jobs without giving them a two week notice, but I did not want to stay alone with Kendrick either. I was betwixt on what to do. At this point Ivan, the guy who had been sharing a semi truck with Dad, was showing some interest in me. He had been at the house several times the first few weeks after Jonathon was born. He was actually comfortable holding a newborn baby. One time when Ivan was holding Jonathon the diaper leaked all over Ivan, but he just laughed. Ivan's acceptance of Jonathon really touched my heart, and I put my guard down. He was the kind of guy that really liked helping people, and I could tell he wanted to help me out. He asked me out for dinner, but with all the turmoil going on with my parents I said, no.

I worked a few more times, but it was just to hard to line up a babysitter. I gave my notice at both places. It took me less that a week to get organized and move all of mine and Jonathon's belongings to Cedarfield. I was excited to be with Mom, Grandpa, and Holly.

Chapter 13

After settling in at Grandpa's house my top priority was to make sure Jonathon was on Medical Assistance and WIC. I went to Social Services so that all my information could be transferred. Social Services needed more information on the baby's father and sent me to Child Support. The man in that office was fed up with dead-beat dads and unwed moms. He was rude and mean to me. He told me I should have just aborted my baby. I had no right to raise a baby and expect the government to pay for it. He told me I was just a burden on society. I was crushed, devastated at such cruelty. I cried for days after that appointment. I was just trying my best to figure out a way to make ends meet and support my baby. I just wanted a little help.

Ivan, the guy that drove truck with Dad, started calling me in Cedarfield. His divorce was done, and his ex-wife had left town. They had abandoned all plans of reconciliation. He wanted to take me out to dinner. He was in the area, often hauling loads of potatoes. After he dropped his load and parked the truck he called me to come pick him up so we could go out for dinner. This started happening a couple times a week. In October he asked if I would come up to his house for a weekend. I was so thrilled with the attention and acceptance, I really thought that no one would ever be interested in someone like me.

That first weekend I went up north with him we put Jonathon in his car seat and packed him in between the seats in the semi. I was so happy to have someone willing to love me and my baby, I smiled the whole trip.

We had a really nice weekend, and to my surprise on Sunday morning Ivan turned on the television to watch some TV evangelist.

I was really intrigued with all that the man had to say I could tell he knew a lot about the Bible, and he spoke as if Jesus talked to him like a friend.

The next couple weeks I would travel back and forth between Cedarfield and Otter Bay. I met all of Ivan's family and had Christmas with them. I really liked what I saw, a big happy family all enjoying a holiday together. The best part being that they accepted me as if I belonged and was part of the family. I never remember having any happy Christmases as a kid since my parents usually worked and fought over how and what the traditions would be. It was a very emotional time of year for me.

Ivan asked if Jonathon and I would come live with him. It did not take me long to move all of my and Jonathon's things into the house in Otter Bay. I really enjoyed getting to know Ivan's family, and his sister-in-law Margie really took me under her wing. One of the first things she did was invited me to go to a ladies night in Heron Creek with her. Ivan said he would watch Jonathon, and I could go ahead and go to the Finnish Sauna with the gals. I had a great time, getting back to the house around ten o'clock. Jonathon was sleeping, so I did not wake him.

I did have to get up at four in the morning, because my dad was giving me a ride to Cedarfield. I had a WIC appointment at ten a.m. He was heading that way with the semi, and it would save me gas money. Jonathon stayed asleep when I moved him to his car seat. As soon as we got to Cedarfield I gave Jonathon to my mom to watch and took off for my appointment.

When I returned my parents were both very upset and showed me that Jonathon had a bruise the size and shape of a man's hand on his butt and a few fingerprints on his upper chest and back. I went hysterical and asked them what I should do. I am not sure who and how, but I did end up at the emergency room so that I could make sure that Jonathon was okay. I did not know about the law that if there is suspect of abuse the hospital must report it to the police. The police came and questioned me, and I told them what I knew. When I finally talked to Ivan he said that he had Jonathon in the shower and the baby had slipped, almost falling to the tub floor. He was unaware of any bruises; he had only grabbed him to stop him from getting hurt. I did not believe it deep down inside, but I also did not want to rock the boat in this relationship that promised provisions, acceptance, family, and a place to live.

Together we attended a Lutheran Church in town regularly. I went to a Bible study with Ivan's mom and really tried to learn more about God. One time at the Bible study a scripture was read that used the word, "sepulcher." I had never heard of the word before and asked what it meant. All the ladies started to laugh at me, not believing I did not know that the word meant "tomb." I learned not to ask questions there anymore.

I did make one good friend at this church. Her name is Sophie. Her little red-headed handicapped daughter stole my heart the first time I met her. Jewel was five at this time, and her other daughter was seven. Her husband worked for Ivan's uncle.

In May Ivan asked me to marry him, and I said yes. Wedding plans began quickly. We picked a date at the end of August. He decided who would stand up in the ceremony: his two sisters and ex-sister-in-law, two ex-brothers-in-law and my brother Brody. I was hurt that my friend Holly could not stand up too. I had just stood up in her wedding the fall before. I just did not want to cause any friction; I only wanted to be loved and accepted.

Dad already had had several different girlfriends, and one with two teenage children had moved in. Funny thing is, she had been married to Ivan's cousin and had the same last name as the one I was gaining in marriage.

Margie, my sister-in-law, helped with many of the plans. She was always talking about Jesus and how he should be part of my everyday life. I did not understand but began to trust her. She offered to play the organ at our wedding. She was tickled when I asked if her youngest daughter would be our miniature bride.

One day Margie asked me to go along with her to Heron Creek to pick up some music. We went to a lady's house whose name was Lily. This lady loved dogs, crafts, and kids, but most of all she loved Jesus, and it was obvious by her speech and actions. I found out that she and her husband had moved to the area from Iowa to help with a drug-rehab ministry. Her husband was a pastor of a small non-denominational church that Margie, her husband (Ivan's brother), and their six kids attended. When I shared my name she said that she had heard of me before. When she was at a Bible study a few years earlier one of my teachers was there too and asked for specific prayer for me. We instantly became friends.

Chapter 14

A few weeks before the wedding I received a call on the phone in which the first words I heard from this unfamiliar voice were, "Are you sitting down?"

I quickly sat down as my heart began to pound. My first thoughts were that something had happened to Grandpa, but the words I heard were, "I am your dad, and I want to meet you." Wow, what a shocker!

Trembling I said, "Sure, when and where?" He said he was in the area and would like to come to my home.

Within twenty minutes he was there, and his first words were, "Oh my God, you got my nose!" It was very awkward, but he came in, met Jonathon, and we talked a short while. Then he said he had to leave, and he did, but fifteen minutes later called back and said he would like to take Jonathon and me out to lunch. He picked us up and took us to town, where we had a pleasant lunch together. I filled him in on my life. He told me a little about his wife and place in Kentucky, and that his name was Clifford, but not much more.

I wanted to invite him to my wedding, but I was terrified inside, as I did not know how my dad, Kendrick would handle it. All I could remember was that he kept a loaded pistol on top of our refrigerator when I was young. I figured he probably would have used it to kill Clifford if he ever showed up at our house or tried to harm me.

Clifford went to Cedarfield before going back to Kentucky and bought me some nice clothes and beautiful jewelry. He dropped the gifts off at my mom's house, and then my mom got the gifts to me. I quickly wrote him a thank-you note and dropped it in the mail. The day it arrived he called me and told me that he had not told his wife about me yet and was glad he got the mail that day. She usually got the mail, not him. I promised him I would not write again until he called and told me it would be okay.

He would frequently call me and just say, "I love you," and then hang up. He did ask if he could come to my wedding, and I said it would be okay, but he would have to keep a low profile.

The wedding was in the Otter Bay community building, and we were married by the pastor of the Lutheran Church. The thought kept coming to me that there might be a murder at my wedding, but I knew there was nothing I could do about it.

Clifford came to my house with my mom the morning of the ceremony so we could spend a little time together. He wanted to meet Ivan, but Ivan was so hungover that every time he stood up to meet my dad, he would run to the bathroom and vomit. What an awful first impression he made. I was embarrassed. I was not sure if my husband-to-be would make it to his own wedding. Good thing it was in the afternoon.

At this point I also realized that my dad had a drinking problem. That morning the ice in his glass melted so I dumped it into the sink to give him some new ice and water. Wow, did he let out a holler! "That's not water; it's vodka in my glass!" I did not realize he was drinking at that time of the morning. He promised to sneak into the wedding late and leave early; he was good for his word.

I went off the pill on our wedding day, did not have a period in September, had one in October and got pregnant in November. We did not have any insurance, and Ivan could not work at driving truck anymore because he had herniated a disc in his back. To help ease the pain and get his back to heal, we began driving sixty miles round trip, three times a week for chiropractic treatments. This was covered by his work insurance. I was so thankful that I had no complications with this pregnancy. I had a great local doctor who was a family practitioner. The nice part was he understood that we could not afford insurance, so he was willing to barter labor on his house from Ivan for payment for his services.

Chapter 15

At some point during this time Dad told Raquel, his wife, about me, and she and I began a phone relationship. It was great to get to learn more about each other. We really bonded in a special way. Raquel was excited when I found out I was pregnant, as she was unable to have kids and had just lost a baby a short time before. Our Christmas present from them was round-trip tickets to their place in Kentucky.

The trip started out a bit amiss, as the airport did not have record of us in the computer. When it finally came through we had missed the connecting flight. The airlines flew us to Chicago and put us up in the Hilton for the night. The next day we made it to Kentucky. It was a very nice Christmas, getting to know Raquel in person, my dad a bit better, and some of Raquel's relatives. They also gave us many gifts, which included maternity clothes for me and toys for Jonathon. Raquel even gave me a shirt that she had got when she was pregnant and had worn a few times. It was a visit filled with love and acceptance.

That winter I was growing larger, mothering Jonathon and babysitting other kids to help bring in some income. Margie and Lily had challenged me to start reading the Bible myself. Lily and her husband started coming over to our house every week to teach us from the Bible. Several other friends joined in on the study too.

Ivan went to work skidding wood for his father. He did not have very much of an income. It was very frustrating not having enough money to live on. I began making lists of what I was believing God to help me with; snow pants and winter clothes for Jonathon, enough money to pay the phone and electric bill, even a microwave. Amazingly God provided it all, and we always had enough food to eat and a roof over our heads.

One cold winter day Ivan's mom called in a panic. She said that Ivan had been in a terrible accident and that I better meet them in town at the doctor's office immediately. She did not tell me what happened or how bad it was, just to hurry.

After bundling up Jonathon and snapping him into his car seat I was off, driving the eight miles to town in a panic. When I arrived I learned that a tree had snapped back on Ivan, and his leg was broke in two places, and he needed multiple stitches. It was too swollen to put a cast on that first day. The doctor recommended a five-thousand-dollar surgery where pins would be put in. I just cried. I said we don't even have enough money to pay for this baby coming; we could never incur a hospital bill like that. We went home trying to figure out what to do and how this could be taken care of. A couple days later, when the swelling had gone down a bit, the doc put a cast on it, and Ivan went back to work.

During that winter we started attending the tiny church that Lily's husband pastored. The church was non-denominational and based their belief system completely on the Bible. He was a minister at a group home for those getting off drug addictions, she, an at-home mom, but sometimes she would work as a substitute teacher. They had three adopted children and took in foster kids, since they were never able to have children biologically. Lily was already becoming my spiritual mother, mentoring me, always making herself available to answer questions about the Bible, pray with me, or give me parenting advice. We spent time together almost daily if not in person at least on the phone.

Ivan and I began to get into The Faith Movement, meeting with a group of people for Bible study and prayer weekly. We were encouraged to spend time daily in the Word and with God, plus to meet together regularly with other believers. We were also told to just believe, and God would heal Ivan's broken leg. So six weeks after the accident Ivan took the cast off, I removed the stitches, and he never had it checked again. What a faith builder! He had no pain, no problems, and no limp.

That summer the two of us were water baptized together in the Hawk River. The church had functions often where we could get together socially just enjoying times of fellowship together. It was also a way of inviting others who may not have known Christ personally over for a good time and exposure to the Love of the Lord. During a special fun day in Otter Bay at a member's house we had hay rides from my brother-in-law Rod, (Margie's husband) cider, caroling, and fellowship. There were many people there from diverse places. I met a few people from other churches. One particular lady comes to mind that I met on the hay ride. It was easy to talk about common ground, as she was pregnant and so was I. We both had a toddler and had been married a short time to someone who was not the father of our child. Little did I know at that time that she was carrying the baby that would become my step-daughter many years later.

By summer I was getting very huge. I taught at a community Vacation Bible School, and everyone was asking if I was due any day. That would send me on an emotional roller coaster, as I had two full months to go.

Ivan decided to start up an old family business that had been sitting idle. He reopened the landscaping business that summer for income. It was in his father and brother's name. I had to go to an accountant for several years to get all the paper work legal and done correctly. All the hours he was gone and as hard as he seemed to work, there was barely enough money to make ends meet. I don't know if he was mishandling the money or just not collecting it. I was glad my mom had taught me to be thrifty, and our new church taught me the law of tithing.

Sometimes I would get overwhelmed with our relationship. One minute Ivan would act nice and kind, as if he were a Christian; the next he was in the bar drinking, cussing, swearing, and chewing like a heathen. I would get very upset at the hypocrisy, and I would want to leave, but I felt I really had nowhere to go. I would just sit and cry, then pray and pour my heart out to God and ask Him to fix the situation. If

I would try to say anything it would turn into a fight and remind me of the turmoil of my childhood, something I wanted to avoid and not raise my children in. My biological dad and Raquel even made a few house payments for us and tried to help as much as they could.

In July I went into false labor three times. My doctor would always be so patient and kind to me. He would say, "When the apple is ready it will fall off the tree."

Chapter 16

Finally, the first week of August the real contractions started. We went over by Margie's and dropped off Jonathon for her to watch. We walked around the horse pasture for a while just to make sure it was the real thing. I called the doctor, around ten o'clock that night, we met in his office. He checked me and said, "This is the real thing. Go right to the hospital in Heron Creek."

Ivan drove the ten miles to the hospital with a few contractions hitting on the way. I checked in and got situated in a room. About ninety minutes passed, and a nurse came in to check me and said that everything was coming along just fine. About thirty minutes later she came in and checked my cervix again. She said, "My, you are moving along rather quickly. I'd better call Doc to come in right away."

It did not take long for him to arrive. As he checked me my water broke in a swoosh, splashing all over him and the floor. He did not even have time to change clothes, and at two a.m. Dillon entered this world. Doc always told me, "Having your first baby is like building a new road, but the second is like repaving it." That was true, as this delivery went very smoothly.

We had chosen the name Dillon for several reasons. One, Raquel, my step-mom had a great nephew with that name, and we really liked it; the other was that it means "faithful." We were learning that God was faithful to us providing a healthy baby and roof over our heads.

I came home the next day. I was tired but happy. Ivan went out to celebrate becoming a father. I was home, watching the two boys, answering the phone for the business, and growing very weak from the blood loss and lack of food. It was getting later and later, and I had no idea where he was, but figuring he was out carousing, I started calling around to the local taverns and finally found him at a bar where he was drinking. I told him that I needed him at home and that I was hungry. When he arrived home he brought me supper, a takeout box full of cold, fried fish and french fries several hours old. I was not a happy camper, but I did not bother to say much, as I knew from my childhood it was useless to argue with a drunk.

I babysat a few kids for some income. I also did all the bookwork for the landscaping business, being careful with what little money we had. I saved money by having a garden and canning and freezing most of our food. I even made a deal with the local vegetable stand. If they had any produce that they were ready to throw out they could just give me a call, and I would take it home. I spent many nights canning tomatoes or freezing strawberries until it was very late, since if I waited until morning the food would be too spoiled to use.

Mom and Kendrick's divorce was finalized this summer too. Mom took over the tavern running it to survive.

I learned to ask the Lord for guidance with the few dollars I had. It was hard on my own to decide if I should use the money to buy toilet paper or if I should go to a nearby potato farm and buy potatoes, since I could get fifty pounds for two dollars there. My faith grew in leaps and bounds as I trusted God to provide everything we needed. I made sure I tithed ten percent of every dollar I earned to show God I trusted Him, and He faithfully provided food for every meal.

Ivan did not want to tithe off of the income from the business, and I think the discourse about that hindered some blessings. We really struggled through the next winter. Ivan worked for his father again, not bringing enough money home to even cover our monthly mortgage payment. The bank began to threaten to take the house away.

I called my dad in Kentucky, and after talking to Raquel he made a few payments on the house for us, enough to get us through the spring and to the opening of the landscaping establishment for the next season. Dad said since it was so hard for Ivan to get a decent job in the winter that we should think about spending the next winter living with them. Raquel liked the idea too.

Ivan had a busy summer landscaping many yards and doing the usual pruning and lawn mowing of such a business. I continued to do all the book work, taking the phone calls, setting up appointments and paying the bills. My cousin Randy worked for us mowing and making deliveries. I taught at the ecumenical Vacation Bible School again, took Jonathon into town for swimming lessons, and both boys to the library program every week.

When fall came I was pretty excited about moving to Kentucky for the winter, not having to deal with cold and snow, but most of all getting to know Raquel and Dad better was a dream come true.

Chapter 17

The little house we had stayed in the Christmas before last was now occupied by a family who was building a house in Dad and Raquel's back yard. Lyle and his wife had a son, Zeke, and were going to have a baby in the spring. Lyle was retired from the Army and stayed home, his wife Corrine was a teacher. We settled into a routine fairly quickly. Dad worked construction and Raquel was a United States Court Clerk. I kept their house clean and did most of the cooking making sure to have a meal ready when they came home each night from work. It was great getting to know Raquel's family, and the best part for me was that they accepted me and made me feel like I belonged in the family.

Raquel and I became closer each day, and I really enjoyed having her as my step-mom. She told me that my dad had a son named Jeremiah that she had never met. It was hard to grasp that I actually had a half-brother somewhere.

My dad seemed to be under the influence often, which made Raquel very unhappy. She could see that my dad's drinking habit was getting worse, as it seemed he was under the influence more often than not. One night she tried confronting him in front of me. The conversation escalated into a fight, this argument made me very uncomfortable. The guilt of not being part of my childhood was eating at him, and Raquel knew it, but Dad was not ready to be confronted about it.

He really tried hard to be a good dad and grandfather, taking Jonathon and me to the circus, changing Dillon's dirty diapers, and letting us help with all the critters on the farm. He just never had a good role model, and the alcohol had a death grip on him.

I was a bit frustrated, as Dad did not offer Ivan any paying work until well into January. Ivan did stay busy; he laid block in the house we were staying at for the fireplace and put a patio in for Raquel's sister and brother-in-law. Ivan was getting frustrated, too, but would not say anything to my dad. Once he finally got to work he would get very upset with the guys on the construction crew because every time the temperature would dip below forty-five degrees the guys said it was too cold to work. He thought that was the ideal temperature to do physical labor in.

I stayed busy with the boys and keeping the folks' house up. I really missed having a church family and prayed for a place to go. This was the Bible Belt there were churches everywhere. Every time I passed a huge pole building church on the side of the highway called L'vie. I had an inner urging to go there. It was located a couple miles from the house. I talked Ivan into trying it, yet I had some fear of what we would be getting ourselves into. We walked in there totally relying on God that we would fit in ethnicity wise and that it would be a place that would teach God's word. Once there I realized it was God who put the idea of attending there in my heart, as it was a fully Bible-based church with special services during the week for kids and adults. I began attending so much that Raquel once observed, "You really like to go to church."

I said, "I sure do." I am not sure if she ever understood, but I know between the church and the daily Christian radio I listened to I was growing in leaps and bounds. The show, *Rafael's Coffee Shop,* challenged me to fast, take daily communion, and walk daily, hand in hand with Christ, feasting on his word.

I had my first experience at this time where God gave me a word for someone else. It was a bit unnerving for me because I felt it might be wrong or something I had made up myself. This thought came into my head to write Habakkuk 2:2-3 on a card. It read, "Then the Lord answered me and said: Write the vision and make it plain on tablets, that he may run who reads it. For the vision is yet for an appointed time;

But at the end it will speak, and it will not lie." I had not even heard of the book of Habakkuk before. I then felt like I should give it to Pastor Bennett. He graciously accepted it and said it was a word in due season. I realized I had heard from God and obeyed.

I also really grasped the message of forgiveness while I was in Kentucky. I was confronted with the word from many sources so I am not sure when the light really went on that I needed to forgive everyone that had ever hurt me in the past, anyone I had even the slightest grudge against. I knew the Lord's Prayer and the words, "Forgive us our trespasses as we forgive those who trespass against us."

It was clear that God could not forgive me any more than I forgave others. I started a list writing down everyone I could think of who had ever hurt me. As I started to think of the things they did to me the tears flowed down my cheeks. I began to pray, "Lord, they don't deserve to be forgiven. They did terrible things to me." As I continued to look at the truth in the Bible I knew I had to let this go. Finally I prayed, "Lord, I know they don't deserve it, and I really do not want to forgive them, but I want to please You even more. I want to do what You say is the right thing to do. Please help me!" A release rushed in. I knew I had finally let go of the offenses committed to me.

Chapter 18

In the spring we headed back to Minnesota to run the landscaping business for another summer. We also started adoption proceedings so that Ivan could become Jonathon's legal father. I had a health-issue scare, with a bad pap, leading to several bad paps, a biopsy, and removal of precancerous cells on my cervix. A combination of answered prayer and medical procedures took care of the situation. Doc was always good about letting us barter for his services and doing as much as possible in his office instead of sending us to the hospital. A great thing about living in a small rural community. Time went on but our finances did not get better.

Death seemed to be surrounding me at this time of my life. Ivan's grandma died unexpectedly. She came down with the flu for two or three days and then was gone. This really devastated me, as she and I had become very close over the years. We spent time together almost daily. I ended up helping Ivan's grandfather out quite a bit. He was unable to take care of himself. Dementia was setting in. I made sure he had meals or had a ride into town for Senior Citizen meals. He eventually ended up in a nursing home.

Also during this season in my life my step-mom Raquel found out she had colon cancer and had to start treatments right away. I called every week. The week of treatment she was too weak to talk or eat. The second week after treatment she was feeling a bit better. By the third week after treatment she would start to feel like herself. She remained positive and would tell me that she was going to "beat this damn cancer." Then it was time for another round of treatments. This cycle happened a few times.

In June my dad called and begged me to come down and help, as Raquel was not doing well at all. He promised to pay for my ticket but then never sent any money for it. I don't know where I got enough money for a plane ticket but God provided.

Nothing could have prepared me for the shock I experienced when I saw her, my vibrant happy, full-of-life step-mom was a walking zombie who could hardly talk. I was crushed but could not show it. Dad's niece Sally had moved in to help, but all the alcohol Dad was consuming and the horrid pain Raquel was in made for a dysfunctional mess. No one agreed what was best or where she should go. I just wanted to escape, run away from the whole mess. I felt helpless and missed my boys. I fumbled through those two weeks trying not to show my emotions, trying to pray, and trying to just stay out of the way. I felt so completely useless and alone. I was losing someone who had accepted me. I left the day after Raquel went back in the hospital for the last time. I never saw her alive again. I could not afford to return for the funeral.

My mom had moved out of Grandpa's house and rented a house with her new boyfriend, Sid. They had known each other since they were children. He was actually a first cousin to Kendrick's first ex-wife.

Shortly after that crushing blow my grandpa came down with colon cancer and was bedridden. Mom and Sid moved in to take care of him. I got to Cedarfield as often as I could. When he died in March I could not have survived without the Lord to lean on. I learned the truth of the scripture in Matthew, "Blessed are those who mourn, for they shall be comforted."

When Grandpa died I thought I was pregnant but had not taken a test yet. I was fine the night of the visitation, but the next morning I started to bleed vaginally. I ended up in the emergency room at Saint Claire's hospital, missing my grandpa's funeral. I became very fearful that I was having a miscarriage. I began quoting scripture out of the Bible, I said Deuteronomy 28:2 "And all these blessings shall come

upon you and overtake you, because you obey the voice of Your God."
also verse four in chapter 28, "Blessed be the fruit of your body...."
The doctor said it was a sore on my cervix that had popped, nothing
more. I then asked if he thought I was pregnant, and he said he was
not allowed to say, but that when a woman is pregnant her uterus looks
blue, and that mine sure looked blue. That helped ease the pain a bit.
I had an empty spot that I did not get to finish my goodbye to Grandpa.

I also had to deal with a hollow feeling that he may have not
accepted Jesus as his personal Savior even though I asked Grandpa
and Raquel each individually to ask Jesus into their hearts. Eerily they
both replied in very much the same way, "No, I am too much of a
sinner." That has left a huge ache in my heart.

Chapter 19

That summer Ivan ran the landscaping business, and I continued to do all the book work and scheduling. My brother Brody worked for us that year. He and his wife Jennifer had moved to Otter Bay from Oklahoma. They had their first baby, Phoebe, that summer as I grew bigger with my third child. Jonathon's adoption went through, and Ivan became his legal father.

In the autumn we realized that we were not going to be able to keep the house. The bank had started foreclosure, and my dad was in no position to help us anymore. We needed a new place to live, fast. Ivan's grandpa had been in the nursing home, and the old farm house was sitting empty. Ivan got permission from his family for us to move in there.

I made the best of a very bad situation. There was barely any running water, there was no septic, the upstairs ceiling had collapsed and was on the floor molding, the plumbing fixtures in the bathroom had been tied off with old rags, and the wall and some windows had been patched with cardboard. It would take a lot to make this place livable before the baby came. I started with the kitchen, pulling cupboard doors off and drawers out. The many years of Irma's donut frying days were very obvious by the amount of grease layered on the wood and the number of maggots that were living in it. I had to soak everything in ammonia and take a wire brush and scraper to it. Eventually things were clean enough for paint. I chose two tones of blue and a cheap contact paper to put on the walls between the cabinets. We paneled the other walls. The molding walls and cardboard were removed, and pieces of new drywall were added. We moved in at the end of October. It was not perfect but livable. I got the baby stuff ready, and the boys settled in. I had to figure out how to haul all my wash water out by hand after using it several times and how to use as little water as possible, since the well barely worked, and there was no septic. I was always amazed at how God faithfully helped me so much with just day-to-day survival.

Chapter 20

On the last Sunday of November, labor began. We met Doc in town, and he said, "You better go to the hospital, with all the snow, the distance to travel, and considering how fast your last labor went." We dropped the kids by Ivan's folks and headed to Heron Creek.

Once in the hospital we called Lily, who I had invited to watch the birth. She had never been able to bear children, and I felt as if she was a mother to me, being very comfortable with her presence there. I knew Lily would be praying and very supportive.

The contractions continued to get stronger and closer, but my cervix would not open. We walked the halls all of Monday and Tuesday, but my cervix refused to budge. It reminded me of labor with Jonathon. Ivan became pretty angry because it was the middle of deer-hunting season, and he could not be out slaying venison. Lily came and went, as she needed to work and get some sleep.

The thought finally occurred to me that maybe the cauterization that had been done when I had the precancerous cells removed had something to do with my cervix not opening. I asked the doctor what he thought, and he agreed. Doc decided that on Tuesday night at nine o'clock he would put me on a labor-inducing drug called pitocin. Within fifteen minutes the contractions got stronger. He had to manually stretch my cervix during each contraction, but things really began to move quickly.

By two a.m. Wednesday we had a very healthy baby girl, my dream come true and a promise fulfilled by God. I had only shared with one person that I truly felt that God had promised me a little girl that would glorify him. Holly reminded me of that as soon as she heard the good news.

On Thursday, Thanksgiving Day, I came home from the hospital, basking in the beautiful weather and so very happy for all that God had provided. A few relatives came over for a visit to see the newborn Rachel, named after my step-mom Raquel, which is Rachel in Spanish.

On Friday I felt good and the weather was so lovely I walked over to Margie's and asked her to saddle up a horse for me to ride just so I could say I rode a horse two days after giving birth I didn't ride very far, but I can brag that I did it.

Chapter 21

The next year I stayed very busy with the three kids, babysitting, pursuing my relationship with Christ through Bible studies, daily prayer, and church, and keeping house. I tried to never let a day go by that I did not at least read the Psalms. Someone taught me a neat way to read five Psalms a day according to the day of the month. There is one Proverb for each day, too. I was always trying to make the house a home by doing little things as I could afford it. I even sold handmade crafts of beaded scarves, key chains, and cards at a local craft shop to bring in some income. I did have a nagging feeling that I was never doing enough for God, not following the law close enough. I was struggling with self-esteem issues, and even though I reached a point where I could say, "Jesus loves me," I could not get that idea to transfer to my heart to the point where I really knew that He did.

I had a little bout with mastitis, but with prayer and medicine it went away. Money was very tight, but God always provided. The following winter when Rachel was nearing the age of two I was getting pretty unhappy that she was still in our room and that the upstairs was not finished for the boys to sleep up there. After some pleading I convinced Ivan to finally get some of it fixed and some insulation in so that I could move them up to the second floor. I was glad that I could move Rachel to her own room, hoping she would finally sleep through the night.

Dillon started to have breathing, snoring, and speech problems from swollen adenoids and tonsils. Something needed to be done medically. We were able to get help from a grant for people with no insurance through the hospital for him to have surgery and get them removed. I noticed Ivan was acting unusually strange when all that occurred. He did not even want to come to the hospital and gave me a hard time that he had to watch the two other kids while I spent the night at the hospital with Dillon. I did not need a bad attitude from my husband; having my son go through surgery was emotional enough. God provided a Christian nurse to take care of Dillon. She listened to me, prayed with me, and visited with me on her break time.

A week or so went by after the surgery, enough time for Dillon to be healed well enough to go back to school. I was going about my usual routine and Penny called to say she was running late and would not get Taylor to my house to babysit as early as expected. I said, "That's fine," and then told her I was trying to figure out why the house had such a strange smell. I said, "It smells like burned cauliflower, and I don't know why."

She asked if I had a wood fire going, and I said, "Of course; that is all we use to heat the house." She wondered if I could have a chimney fire. I said, "I suppose it is possible." I went upstairs and felt between the loose insulation and the old decrepit chimney, and said it was very hot and making a crackling sound.

She said that her husband, a volunteer fire fighter could come over and look at it. I said that would probably be a good idea. I kept cleaning my house, not thinking anything much of the possible fire or the possibility of carbon monoxide being there. Before I knew it the whole fire department, lights sirens, and all, were pulling in. I led them to the basement, warning them to watch out for the last step that flipped over if stepped on wrong. I was very embarrassed of the dirt floor with the caving-in stone basement walls.

The firemen quickly ushered the baby and me out the door saying the chimney was plugged. There was a fire in it, the house was full of carbon monoxide. The wood stove had to be dismantled. I stood out in the cold with the baby, watching them take pieces of duct work out the back door, with smoke everywhere.

Ivan and a couple guys that worked for us came rushing into the house, from where I do not know. He started to give me a tongue lashing that was so crude I will not even repeat it. He chewed me out in front of the employees, calling me names, and telling me how stupid I was to call the fire department. He would not listen to me that I did not call them. Then the firemen explained how the whole thing was hooked up wrong, as a furnace and wood stove can not be vented through the same hole in the chimney. Ivan, being a mason, knew this but never shared it with me. I was crushed that he did not even care that the baby and I could have died during the whole episode. He was just very mad that he got caught with a flue hook up that was not up to code. I went to his parents' house to get out of the cold. Later he showed up and started yelling at me again.

After the smoke and carbon monoxide were cleared out we were allowed back in the house. Since the fire was contained in the chimney there was little damage in the house. Ivan hooked up the ancient furnace, and life proceeded "as usual," except that I felt very sick every time it kicked in. I began to wonder if I and the baby could be getting poisoned by carbon monoxide. I asked Ivan to have it checked, and again he was very nasty to me and said, "There is nothing wrong with it." I persisted, even though I preferred to avoid conflict at almost any cost, but with much prayer I knew that I could not let this go. It was a life-and-death situation.

He finally said, "Fine, just call someone." So I looked up a local furnace business in the phone book and placed a call. They came out right away and checked the furnace. I was so thankful that one of my friends was at the house for a visit because she heard what the guy said and was my witness. He told me that the furnace was leaking carbon monoxide, and that he had to tag it. He wished he did not have to, but if we died after he checked it he would be held liable. With no heat in the house I started making phone calls to get a hold of Ivan and tell him what was going on. When I eventually reached him he once again chewed me up one side and down the other saying that the furnace guy didn't even know what he was talking about and was just trying to sell me a new furnace. Then he went on to accuse me of sleeping with the furnace guy. I did not even understand how that statement fit into the conversation. I was crushed realizing he did not care if we died.

I called Lily, and we decided the best thing to do would be to get out of the house for a few days. Lily said the kids and I could stay at her house. When I told her I really needed some quiet time to seek God and get direction, she offered me a cabin to stay in. She took care of the place and could use it whenever she needed to. She would watch the kids for me, too.

I spent the next three days fasting, praying, and seeking God's face. The words that came to me ever so clearly were; "Get out of that house, or you and your children will die." I shared this with Dave and Lily, and they said they would do whatever was needed to help.

Chapter 22

Lily worked for a crisis intervention program and was able to get a place in a local motel with efficiency apartments for the kids and me to live in temporarily. It took much courage on my part, but I knew the kids and I would die if I did not obey. I got up that morning sent Jonathon and Dillon off to school telling them I would pick them up at the end of the day. Next I packed a few belongings of mine and the kids, strapped the baby in the car seat and into the truck and drove to town, sobbing. I did not take much, as I truly believed that Ivan would see the danger and would fix the furnace, then soon we would all be back together and could celebrate Christmas as a family.

The kids did not mind the adventure of the one-bedroom apartment. The boys were excited about the holidays. I had some contact with Ivan and invited him to the boys' school Christmas concert. Ivan said he had other plans and would not be able to come with us.

A few days later Ivan showed up at the motel apartment to see the kids. He informed me that he had found an apartment for the kids and me to live in. It was in town, and he had already spoken to the owner. We could move upstairs of the gift shop right away. That week he helped us move and brought the cats and the Christmas tree from our home for me to take care of. During this time I could not sleep or eat, just cry, pray, listen to praise tapes, or read my Bible. I lost an alarming amount of weight. I looked anorexic.

Sophie gave me a set of bunk beds for the boys that her girls had outgrown. Rachel and I shared a rolling cot that came with the apartment. The appliances were furnished. Ivan started driving truck for the farm again, something I had been begging him to do for the past few winters so we could have enough money for groceries. I had to go to work to support the kids, so I started waitressing at a supper club attached to the motel we had just lived at.

Less than two weeks after settling into the apartment, Kendrick, my adoptive dad, called and said he had something very important to share. Ivan had just called him and asked to be dropped off at some lady's house and confessed to my dad that he had a girlfriend. I was so shattered there are no words to describe the pain. I had really believed that everything was going to work out. How could it when Ivan had already moved in with a girlfriend?

I did not want to give up hope. I did not want my children to go through the pain of their family being ripped apart from divorce. I just wanted a safe place to live and to make amends with my husband. I wanted him to love me and not abandon me. I wanted him to accept me and not reject me. I did my best not to argue or fight with him. I would let him come over to my apartment whenever he wanted.

I even let him drop off his dirty laundry, and I would wash his clothes for him. I had to haul it all down a flight of steps and drive a few blocks to the Laundromat, but I thought it would help bring him back. I would invite him over for dinner. He was very inconsistent, and I never knew when he would show up. Sometimes he said he would be right over when he called, so I would tell the kids, "Daddy is coming for a visit," but then he would not show up. It was very confusing and heart wrenching for not only me but the three kids also.

Chapter 23

One night I was up praying my heart out, and God showed me a vision of a beautiful castle. I don't want to sound overly spiritual and wish there were better words to describe this. It was not some mystical happening but more like a thought in my mind. This castle was made of blocks that were crystal clear and reminded me of the ice castle in Heron Creek. In my mind I asked, "What is it, Lord?"

Then I heard in my mind, "It is the marriage that I will build for you. It will not be built of worldly materials but of pure gold that is perfectly clear because all the imperfections are removed."

Wow! I was so excited that God would talk to me. Now I really wanted to know if God meant this marriage would be with Ivan, not even letting myself think it could possibly be with anyone else. When I said, "Lord, will this castle-like marriage be with Ivan?" I did not get an answer. I just assumed then that it would be and continued to believe that God would rebuild my marriage and a reconciliation would happen.

I really knew that God was answering my prayers when Ivan agreed to go to a counseling session. We set a date to meet with Dave and Lily at their house. This really gave me hope that a healing of our marriage was on the way.

The night the counseling session was to happen I had thought he might not even show up; my heart began to sink, but he did eventually arrive late. While we were waiting Lily had her television set on, tuned into a lady preacher with a husky, truck-driver voice. I liked what she was teaching about the Bible.

Dave sat us down and asked me, "Shelby, what do you want from Ivan?"

I said, "For him to stop seeing this other woman and work on our marriage."

Dave asked Ivan what he thought of that. He replied, "No way. I will not stop seeing her."

Dave said, "Then I guess there is nothing else left to do."

Ivan got up and left. All my dreams and hopes of us getting back together were smashed. I cried and cried some more. That night I knew in my heart my marriage was over. I sobbed for days with intense pain. The best way I could describe it was as if someone would have physically dug their fingertips into my skull and ripped my body in half. I felt that even that kind of pain would have been less than what I was experiencing.

During those years that I was living in poverty with Ivan the little church we had been attending merged with another small church to create another non-denominational church. Dave was now an assistant pastor, and Greg was the pastor. This tiny church was very supportive of the kids and me, offering money, a car, prayer, and help with the kids.

Chapter 24

My mom really wanted me to come to Cedarfield, but she understood that I could not take the only two consistent things my kids had out of their lives. I would not allow their school or church to be ripped from them, too. As it was, most of their toys, clothes, and everything they had known were gone. Ivan refused to give us our personal possessions, saying that since I was the one who moved out I did not deserve any of it.

I knew I could not make ends meet by only waitressing. I prayed; God answered. People came to me and asked if I would work for them. I began to clean private homes during the week days and cabins on Saturdays. I also was offered a job to help with bookwork at a business during the late mornings and early afternoon. I continued to waitress but switched to a different restaurant. One night Ivan was cruel enough to bring his girlfriend in for me to wait upon. The owner let me hide out in back, and she took care of them.

I cleaned most days, worked in the office most afternoons, and waitressed in the evenings. I took Tuesdays and Sundays off to be with my kids. I would work Sunday nights; I passed up the big tips of Sunday brunch to go to church. Most of the people I worked with could not understand why I would give up such an easy way to make extra money, but I knew that the emotional and spiritual support that the kids and I would get at the church was worth more than money.

The first week of April a prophet visited the church and had this to speak over me; *"Our sister on the back corner back there, there has been some battles. What's your name, honey?"*
I replied, "Shelby."

"Stand up. God wants to touch you. Are you married?"
I replied, " I am in the process of a divorce."

"Yes, I just wish you would not have even told me that. I saw a real problem, a bad tough relationship and all kinds of stuff, and I hear the Lord saying, 'I have a new day for you.' The fire of God wants to touch you. Come up here, honey. God wants to touch you. Let me tell you something; He sent His word and healed and delivered them from their destructions. God wants to renew your spirit. God wants to heal your heart. God wants to touch you afresh and anew.

"I'm telling you God's gonna heal the bruised. How many know bruises are some of the toughest things? Oh, God's gonna heal a bruised heart here tonight. God's gonna put faith in your heart, and I'm telling you that depression that's tried to take hold of you and take you down, you've even thought of some crazy things, but God's gonna set your face like a flint. You're not gonna be moved. In the name of Jesus. Lord, touch her. We thank you for healing my sister now, in the name of Jesus.

"God is gonna do some rewiring within you, honey. You're wired for 110, but He's gonna rewire 220 inside of you. And there're some things inside of you that have caused you to think a certain way that have opened you up to get hurt, not once but many times.

"You've been in a cycle, and the Lord says, 'It's time to stop this cycle. It's time we don't go around this mountain anymore. It's time to break the yoke of bondage the enemy tried to put on you, even when you were a little girl,' saith the Lord. That when he'd come in and hurt you. The Lord says, 'I was there, and I've brought you even to this day, that I would bring a deliverance,' saith thy God. 'And I set you free, even this hour for it is a new day.' The Lord says, 'Know this. I am doing a work of grace.' Lift your hands toward her right now, in the name of Jesus. We command you foul thing that has tried to destroy my sister, you can't do it anymore. We command you to back off and let her go now. in Jesus name.

"The Lord says, 'I'm going to quicken you, and I'm gonna do a work in you. Hold fast,' saith the Lord, 'I will be thy bridge over troubled waters.' And the Lord says, 'You will not be as the disciples in the midst of the storm, when they felt like they were gonna sink, but surely was I out there,' and thus saith the Lord, 'for I appeared, and we were on the other side. We're goin' to the other side, and I'm gonna be your provision and your strength.'

"The Lord says, 'It's not over until I say it's over. I've got a few things you haven't thought of yet. But I'm gonna move, and you're gonna see a miracle on your behalf,' saith the Lord And the Lord says, 'Don't fear provision; don't fear,' for God's got his plan to take care of you in the name of Jesus.

"There is a time of intercession. God is calling you to intercession. You've heard the cry not just once. I see the Lord waking you in the night, calling you to come apart. You don't need to go to the bathroom, and you don't know why you wake up. God's calling you to get up and get alone and get in that closet, honey, and He's gonna sit down there with you and meet with you, and I'm telling you, you won't just be saying verbal prayers. I'm telling you, you're gonna be in the Shekinah Glory of God, and the Glory of the Lord is gonna descend on you, and He's gonna minister to you. He's bringing you into the inner chambers of the Lord. Therefore, hearken to the Word of the Lord.

"When He knocks go to Him; go to Him. There's times when intimate things take place with the Lord and nobody else is allowed. You're gonna find yourself in the crowds and on the phone and doing things, and you'll hear the call of God saying, 'You're mine; you come to Me, and you get alone and spend time.'" 'And the Lord's gonna begin to do some healing in your heart, and there's some things even from your youth, and He's *doing a rewiring in you, honey, and a renewing in your heart, and God's gonna do a new thing inside of you. Lift up your hands to the Lord. God's putting His anointing on you.*

"Now we thank you, Father, we thank you for the breath of God, thank you for the quickening of the Holy Ghost. Take a deep breath, honey. In the name of Jesus cast that care unto the Lord. It is time for peace, time for rest, rest in the Lord, Amen. Our God reigns."

This prophecy really gave me hope and helped me retain my focus on God.

Since the kids and I lived in the upstairs of a gift shop we had to climb a set of stairs and walk across a roof to get into the house. One day Rachel, just two years old, disappeared. I started searching for her. I heard her crying, "Mommy!" I went running outside. She had fallen off the roof edge and was on a tiny, decorative window ledge almost a full story above a cement sidewalk. I reached down and pulled her up, comforting her and keeping myself together. She told me that an angel had come along and was holding her there, keeping her from falling.

A very hard part of this whole situation was seeing the kids get all excited that their dad was going to pick them up and take them somewhere, but many times he would not show up and not even call to explain his absence. The four of us would just sit together and sob, often, as there were no words that would help.

There were a few times that Ivan did take the kids, but this was very hard on me emotionally. I wondered if they would be safe. Would he treat Jonathon differently? I did try to make the best of any time the kids were gone to draw closer to God. There was one particular time when I was home alone, and I just kept singing to the Lord the song, "You are more precious than silver, more beautiful than diamonds, more costly than gold, but nothing in this world compares with You!" I became totally surrendered to God's will, knowing that is what He wants most. I kept letting go of myself and felt a peace come that everything would be fine, no matter what I faced.

Late in April the owner of the apartment we were living in said that we had to move out by May. He was concerned that there was no place for the kids to play in the summer, and the parking lot could not be a playground.

I continued to saturate myself in God's word with tapes of praise and teaching every waking moment. A confidence that God would take care of me was starting to develop as our relationship grew. The idea that God loves me and accepts me as I am started to settle in my heart.

Within days I was informed that a house was for rent a few blocks from where we were living. I could afford the rent, it was close to school, and each of the kids would have their own room. There was a great yard for the kids to play in, too! It was large and possibly the oldest house in town. It had even been used to film a movie in.

Chapter 25

I picked a day to move and found out what would be the best day to get a crew of guys together to help. The moving day was set for early May a group of men from church came over and helped me move my few things.

I also planned on going to Ivan's and getting the rest of my stuff, since I had a court order that was covered in the separation papers. I had informed Ivan several times on the date and time we were coming. I had it put in the church bulletin, too. I decided to ask a local cop to come along since I had legal papers, and I was afraid Ivan would not cooperate.

That evening, eight men, including the cop accompanied me to the house. When we drove into the yard there was a small car I did not recognize in the driveway. I figured it was the girlfriend's, and that they were off in his vehicle. I still had a key so I unlocked the front door and walked in. I heard a gal scream from my old bedroom that was just off the living room. The next thing I saw was her running naked for her clothes. She quickly got dressed and ran out the door, getting into the car and driving off.

Ivan went ballistic and started screaming that I could not have anything, that I was the one who moved out. The men tried to reason with him but he was like a madman. The cop was going to call back-up for us, but then he was called to help with traffic control at a bad automobile accident. He had to leave quickly but said he would try to get back as soon as possible.

Ivan physically threw my clothes in the yard scattering them in every direction. I told him I really wanted the chifferobe that my great-grandfather had made so he picked up that huge wardrobe by himself and tossed it into the yard.

The guys collected things as they landed and piled them onto a trailer. The men then asked me if there was anything else that I wanted or that I did not get that was on the legal paper. I said I am supposed to get the washer and dryer that belonged to my grandfather. Ivan refused to let us in. He said that no one was allowed into his house, and he would have us arrested for trespassing if we walked over the threshold.

I gave up, deciding that I did not need anything else. I had my kids, my faith, and my sanity, and that was all I needed. We left, and I was glad to get out of there, as I was very shaken up emotionally.

Kendrick and his friend Mari had some extra appliances, so the men went with me to his farm and picked up a refrigerator and stove, setting it up in my new kitchen.

Rachel and I did not have a bed, but God provided. People were calling me from all different places. One gave me a bunk bed for Rachel's room and then I was asked if I needed a bed. She had friends who wanted to get rid of their solid-oak bedroom set, double bed, and two dressers for one-hundred fifty dollars. They would deliver it to my house from Missouri, and they only wanted me to pay them ten dollars a month for payments. I knew it was God using people to bless me. All my needs were provided for. Aunt Diane gave me her couch and many others blessed me with household furnishings.

I eventually had to hire a lawyer and start the divorce proceedings. At first I thought God would be angry with me, I knew the scriptures say He hates divorce. I also remembered what the church had told me as a child about my parents being sinners. I kept pressing in and eventually received a peace about this, after reading in the old testament where even God had to divorce Israel; Jeremiah 3:8 states, "Then I saw that for all the causes for which backsliding Israel had committed adultery, I had put her away and given her a certificate of divorce...." My husband had committed adultery, and God gave me permission to move on.

It didn't all come at once; it took time to totally let go and give up on my marriage. Many days and nights I felt so tired, lost, helpless and out of control. I would cry and grieve about my dying marriage. I would beg God to change my situation and help me be patient. I just wanted to be loved. I knew I was giving God control of my life, but many times my emotions would control me more. Then the peace would come. I would walk in that a few days, but doubt would enter. I would start wondering if I had prayed enough, done enough; was I even worthy of God's help and love?

One night I was in anguish and just could not sleep. I started searching the Bible for some comfort. I somehow ended up in Isaiah 54, the whole chapter ministered to me, but when I read verses four and five I felt like God had put that in the Bible just for me. "Do not fear, for you will not be ashamed; Neither be disgraced, for you will not be put to shame; For you will forget the shame of your youth, And will not remember the reproach of your widowhood anymore. For your Maker is your husband, The Lord of hosts is His name; And your Redeemer is the Holy One of Israel; He is called the God of the whole earth."

Chapter 26

I sought counsel from the Pastor and his wife also. They helped me see that I was not really in love with the man, but I was "in love" with "marriage" or the idea of being loved and accepted. That was very hard to swallow, but I knew it was true. I just wanted to be loved and affirmed unconditionally, something I had searched for my whole life in many wrong places.

I also felt it necessary to get professional counseling for myself and the kids. With the counselor I wrote my new rules:

It's okay to feel my feelings and talk about them with people if it's safe and appropriate, and I want to.

I can think, make good decisions, and figure things out.

I can talk about and solve my problems.

It's okay to be me, to be who I am.

I can make mistakes, be imperfect sometimes be weak, sometimes be not so good, sometimes be better, and occasionally be great.

It's okay to be selfish sometimes and put myself first sometimes, and say what I want and need.

It's okay to give to others, but it's okay to keep some for myself, too.

It's okay for me to take care of me. I can say no and set boundaries.

It's okay to have fun, be silly sometimes, and enjoy life.

I can make good decisions about whom to trust. I can trust myself. I can trust God, even when it looks like I can't.

I didn't always follow my rules but it was a goal worth working on. My dad, Kendrick, helped quite often during this time, too. He gave me a brand-new vacuum cleaner, gave me groceries, and a little cash whenever he could. One night when I had to take Jonathon to the emergency room, Dad came right over to watch the two younger kids. The doctors thought Jonathon was going to need his appendix out and kept him for the night. I stayed in the hospital with Jonathon while Dad stayed the night.

My dad, Clifford, stopped by for a surprise visit. We went out for dinner and caught a show. He spent the night at my house. I noticed he had to have the television on all night. Later I found out it is quite common for alcoholics to need noise in the room all night in order to sleep. It was nice to see him again, but I could tell he was very lost with Raquel being gone.

Life was a daily struggle of juggling several different babysitters to come watch the kids and working all my jobs. I found out that some of the babysitters were not taking very good care of my kids. One actually bruised Rachel. Another stole money, and one would cancel at the last minute, leaving me in a predicament of who would watch my children while I worked.

I did get some very encouraging letters from church friends. Lily was always good about writing me notes about how pleased the Lord was over my faithfulness and reminded me that I was special. A gal named Celeste reminded me to keep looking straight out of my problems and at Jesus who would guide me out of the problems with His light. Sophie was always there with a listening ear, too.

Many nights I would come home after a long night of waiting tables to spend hours doing dishes and cleaning my house so it was livable. The money always varied from day to day; I was only getting paid two dollars an hour when waitressing, yet the taxes were taken out for minimum wage. God always provided enough to get by between tips and money from all my jobs.

I qualified for some state help and was absolutely amazed at the amount of food stamps I was given. I had no idea how to spend that much money at a grocery store. The ladies at the store would laugh at me, saying they never saw anyone use food stamps so wisely, shopping sales and using coupons.

The summer went by really fast. We were all adjusting to our new lifestyle, yet inside I knew I could not continue cleaning toilets and waitressing the rest of my life. I had heard that there might be help for me at the community college. Just the thought of stepping onto a college campus scared me right down to my inner core.

Chapter 27

One day I was feeling as if I should really find out a bit more about college, so I asked Jared, the owner of a Christian book store if he knew where the college was. He gave me directions, and I headed out toward the college. I was still so intimidated and felt inferior and terrified. I just did not know what to expect. I kept thinking I should just turn around and go home. The thought of taking better care of myself and my children was even stronger.

Once I located the main office, I was sent to the Woman's Equity Resource Bureau, where I met Janet. I began to pour out my story, and she offered me hope and comfort. Between my tears and sobs I knew I was in the right place. She told me about classes that I could take that were made specifically for women like me who had not been in college before but wanted an education. We set up a time for an appointment so I could get enrolled in some displaced homemaker classes that were going to begin in a few weeks.

At one of these classes my eyes were really opened. I was a bit overwhelmed with all the things I needed to do to be a good mom, student, and employee. I was complaining how hard life was. The teacher said, "Then why do you do so much?"

I replied, "Because I have to!"

She said, "No. you don't."

I said, "I sure do!

She returned with, "No, you don't. You just might not like what would happen if you don't do those things." She informed me that I did not "have to" feed, bathe, and take good care of my children. Social Services would probably come take them from me if I didn't, but it was my choice. She really helped me see more clearly that the things I was doing, I chose to do. I heard the saying, "You can choose your action, or you can choose your consequence, but you can't choose both." I have tried to remember that philosophy ever since.

Men started noticing me and giving me attention. I was not going to fall into the habits of my past. It was no longer about me; I now had three children totally dependent on me, and I was not about to let them down. I knew I was not ready to get into a serious relationship of any kind. I had been asked out to dinner by a few different guys and did not mind doing that once in a while, but I wanted to make sure I kept my priorities straight.

Lily shared with me that God really has a heart for single mothers. She shared a story from the Bible about a woman who was a widow with a young son. She was getting ready to cook their last meal and preparing to die of hunger after that. The prophet in the story came knocking on the door and told the women to make him some bread with her last bit of flour and oil. She agreed to give it to him as an offering to God, and from that day until the famine was over; her oil flask or flour barrel never ran out. This encouraged me immensely. Lily went on to share that God had a perfect mate for me; that I must ask and then wait on God. I did tell God that if it was His will to provide me with a husband I would marry again, if not I would stay single. I was extremely cautious not wanting to jump into anything in the flesh.

I do believe that God allowed different men who took me on dates into my life to help me see what I truly needed and what character traits to look for.

One guy was very wealthy, even took me on a date in a limo all the way to St. Paul for a Viking game, but had an alcohol problem; showing me that I needed someone who held a job but was stable and not dependent on chemicals and money for happiness. One said he was a Christian as he was very involved in his church and sang in the choir, but he would say he was coming over for dinner and then not show up or even call; teaching me how important a person's actions are, not just their words. Another was the cop, the one who tried to help me out while getting my belongings at Ivan's. Not only was he a bit too young for me, he was not a Christian and didn't have much of a sense of humor. Both things that were on my wish list for the right man. The other was a very kind guy who always brought me gifts and helped do some repairs and painting around the house; he would come over to play cribbage or just hang around. He was much older than me, not a Christian, and had a drinking problem. He had a very seasonal job.

I had the same rule with everyone that asked me out. I would say, "I cannot afford to go Dutch. You will need to pay for the meal and the babysitter, but most importantly, I will not go to bed with you. If you can follow my rules I will go out to dinner with you." All of them accepted my rules, although a couple did want to see if I had changed my mind about intimacy. They quickly learned I had not.

At this point in time I had made up my mind that I was not going to get myself or my children into a mess. I kept my priorities straight: God, then kids, church, work, and then socializing. Each of those men had something to offer that I wanted, but none had all I had asked God for. I actually made a list of fifty things I wanted in a husband, thinking I could compromise a few if someone even came close to the top twenty or thirty, but God had other plans.

Chapter 28

In August I was excited to take the boys to the county fair. It was their first time to ever go to a fair. Ivan would never let us go, as he felt it was just a waste of money, and there was usually not enough money to spend on such frivolity. I dropped Rachel off at a babysitter's house, and off we went to take in the sights, sounds and smells of a small county fair.

While we were in line waiting to get on the tilt-a-whirl my cousin Justine introduced me to some guy named Benjamin and his six-year-old daughter. I had heard of him before because he was a professor at the college I was just starting to attend. We had never officially met before.

Justine knew him because they were neighbors, and she took care of the little girl in the mornings before school. I politely said, "Hi," but then turned the other way focusing on my boys. I did not really want another man in my life at this time. I had a few weeks to go until my divorce was final, and I just wanted to enjoy my kids. I was getting really excited about the thought of going to college and gaining independence from men, the government or anyone but God.

Chapter 29

In the fall the divorce date came. When Mariam, one of my teachers, and Kendrick found out I was planning on going alone, they joined me for the five minutes in front of the judge where my marriage became officially over. After we walked down those flights of stairs and exited the building I was so emotionally numb I could barely say good-bye to Mariam or my dad. I didn't realize how much it would affect my emotions. I thought I was over the hardest part, so I was not prepared to feel detestation the way I did.

I could not even figure out what to do, so I just decided to go to a department store to walk around and see if a little retail therapy would help. I did buy something, my first pair of high heels, not very high but enough to give me a sense of independence, a sign to me that I was going to stand on my own two feet, with God's help, of course. A little chocolate helped too.

That evening Dave and Lily picked me up to bring me out for dinner and take me to a special meeting at a church fifty miles away. They wanted to make sure I was doing all right, and were amazed that I could not speak the whole evening. They had never seen me without something to say. I just quietly sat in my numbness. I don't even recall what the service was about, but it was comforting to be surrounded by believers.

I started college classes, first completing several non-accredited courses that helped me prepare for the real thing: Taming the Math Monster, Self-Assertiveness, and How to Study. I was ready to take real college courses by the winter semester. I started with two art classes, Drawing, and Design, a class on weather, one on government and another in psychology.

I was honored to receive The Larsen Memorial Scholarship and grants that helped pay for everything. I continued working part time and stayed busy being a mom full time. At this time I was growing in many ways. God was showing me how to completely trust Him and put my confidence in Him. God even used a high-ropes course that I was mandated to take because I was receiving state aid. That day I had learned many more lessons on trust and faith and gained some self esteem. Every little success helped me take another step closer to His plan for my life giving me optimism and assurance.

Early in November another prophet visited our church, and this is what he said to me:

"'Shelby, it is a new day,' saith the Lord. 'You've come a long way,' saith the Lord, 'and the half has not yet been told, but this is a new day and a new way,' saith thy God, 'for I am making the crooked places straight,' saith the Lord, 'because you have reached out to take my hand. Fear not, I want you to know I will be a husband to you,' saith thy God. 'I will provide, and I will nurture you. I will cause the waters of life to come upon you to regenerate you again and again,' saith the Lord. 'I am touching your heart,' saith the Lord, 'to heal you of all brokenness and fear,' saith the Lord. 'There's been already a developing of confidence of faith, but the half has not yet been told, my daughter. I will make you an example, a Godly example in the midst of my people of my restorative power and of those who come from brokenness and submit their brokenness unto me, that they might be healed. Even so,' saith the Lord. 'You will comfort others with a comfort that you are receiving of my spirit,' saith the Lord. 'You will be a comforter to many others. Fear not and even the young, you will touch their lives, and you will be used to help them,' saith the Lord, 'and to bring life to them and even be part of those who will train, and know the Lord is with you.'"

Having these words written down to read over and over again gave me more peace in knowing that God was taking care of me and that I was right where he wanted me to be.

Chapter 30

A few weeks into November I received a call at ten-thirty in the evening while talking to another gentleman. It was Benjamin, the professor my cousin had introduced me to. He said we had met at the fair and that he wanted to talk to me. I said, "Just hang on a minute." I put him on hold and told the other guy that I had to go.

Benjamin later told me that he thought I was going to hang up on him at that moment. I surprised him by returning to him so quickly. He stuttered and stammered and asked for my help saying, "I'm not any good at this."

I had no problem getting the conversation going, which helped calm his nerves a bit. We talked late into the night. We shared our core beliefs and parts of our life stories. He said he would call me back when he returned from Thanksgiving vacation with his family.

It was comforting to know that each of us had done all in our own power to try and save our first marriages, but that the ex-spouses had decided it was over, leaving us with no choice.

When I hung up the phone I clearly felt an inner voice within me say, "He is the one!"

I went to the mirror and said, "But God, I'm not ready for this." I knew enough not to mention that to Benjamin, but I was so happy in the inside that I was giddy, knowing that there was something special about this guy.

I went to Cedarfield with the kids to celebrate Thanksgiving with my mom, her husband Sid, Brody, and his family.

Chapter 31

Benjamin called as promised, and we talked some more. I told him that the church I went to had a themed adult night out the first Friday of every month. Since it was now December I was planning on going that week, and if he would like to go along he could. He quickly said, "Sure," but I wondered if he would have second thoughts when I told him the theme was "Hillbilly Night."

I could hardly wait for Friday to arrive. When the evening for our first date finally came I drove the ten miles to his house, since he lived close to the pastor's house where the party was. When I arrived Benjamin came right out to the driveway to meet me. I was quite a sight in my old high-school overalls covered in patches and embroidery, a straw hat with plastic worms hanging all over. We went inside so I could get the boiled okra and collard greens ready. Benjamin put camouflage marks on his face and tied a piece of rope around his jeans. Off we went to the party.

When we entered the Pastor's house everyone there knew me, and all but two couples knew Benjamin. Everyone was talking and saying that we were the perfect couple and should get married. We kept repeating, "Wait a minute; this is our first date!"

I did find out what happened during those three months when Benjamin and I first met in July and when he finally called me in November. Several people had mentioned me to him and encouraged him to call me. The first person that brought my name up to Benjamin was a counselor from the college Benjamin worked in. I had been taking some classes from his wife, and she had mentioned that she thought we would be a good match, and her husband agreed. The second person was a long-time co-worker of Benjamin's who taught history in the same building; he just happened to be my ex-husband's first cousin and knew me well. The final one was my niece, who was one of Benjamin's students at the time.

He said that every time someone brought up my name the thought of a lady with three kids was a bit overwhelming for him. Yet God was at work in Benjamin's heart. He knew he wanted to find someone who did not want any more kids. It was also important to him that this person would accept him and his daughter as a package deal.

After our first date we decided it would be a good idea to meet the kids and let them get to know each other. We felt that a neutral place instead of our homes would be best, so we made plans to meet at the bowling alley for some fun we could all enjoy.

Chapter 32

When we met at the bowling alley on Saturday afternoon. I entered in with my marbleized league ball, matching bag, shoes and towel, all color coordinated. Benjamin arrived a few minutes after me carrying an old black bowling ball with a silver streak sprayed on by a child and a pair of shoes so old that the bowling alley had sold them for fifty cents. I knew right there that he had a sense of humor; he sure made me laugh. The kids all got to meet each other, and we had a great time. The next day after we both attended our separate churches. Benjamin and Robyn came to my house for lunch and more time together.

Christmas was just around the corner, and Benjamin wanted me to go with him and meet his family. I did not have any definite plans, but I knew my two youngest kids would be with their dad. Jonathon preferred to stay with me. Benjamin's folks welcomed me with open arms. I was able to meet Benjamin's sisters, aunts, brothers-in-law, nieces and nephews, and of course Natasha and Caitlin, his two other daughters.

Benjamin had adopted Natasha shortly after marrying Laura, a single mother. Robyn was born a few years into the marriage. They decided together they did not want anymore children, so Benjamin had a vasectomy. Laura was unfaithful and became pregnant, but although the pregnancy was quite a surprise, Benjamin knew that two wrongs don't make a right. Laura wanted to get an abortion and terminate the pregnancy. Benjamin felt trying to keep the family together and to raise the baby as his own was the best thing to do. After much counsel Laura said she would stay and try to work things out. Benjamin was present for the birth. Caitlin was born on his birthday in 1988. He accepted her as his own, but that was not what her mother wanted. A few months after the baby was born she left the marriage and the kids for Benjamin to raise.

Benjamin was earning his doctorate degree, teaching full time, and raising three children by himself. Laura decided she wanted Natasha and the baby back. She had court orders set up so Benjamin would have to pay her child support. She gave Natasha to her mother to raise, but told Benjamin he could have "the ugly one since he made her anyway."

Chapter 33

We started spending as much time together as possible. He and Robyn lived in Heron Creek. I would often pick up his daughter from the after-school day care and bring her to my house. Benjamin worked evenings, often running the clock at the local high school for the basketball games. Then the six of us could have dinner at my house. Robyn could spend time bonding with my kids while Benjamin was doing his after-school duties.

As the cold weather began to creep in I couldn't keep that big old drafty house heated. There was no venting system, no wood heat, just a floor grate to heat the upstairs. I did not have any time to go out looking for a place to rent. I really needed to move into something smaller and warmer. God came through again, providing just what I needed. One of Jonathon's former teachers called me and asked if I would rent from them if they bought a house for an investment. She said they could keep the rent very reasonable and would do all the shoveling, mowing, and yard upkeep. How could I refuse such a great offer?

Chapter 34

In the weeks ahead they bought a duplex just blocks from where I lived, quickly remodeled it into a three-bedroom home. With help from friends from church and Benjamin, the kids and I moved in. The place was great and had a beautiful view of a field out the back, a fireplace, and was located in a pleasant neighborhood near town.

Benjamin and I spent a few months getting to know each other. I began to think it would be really nice to get married. Living ten miles apart and keeping two separate households was taking a toll on me, especially since I was still working, waitressing, cleaning houses and cabins, plus going to college full time. Benjamin and I talked about it, but he said he was not ready yet. He knew there were still too many issues to work out. Where would we all live? Would the kids all go to the same school? What church would be best for all of us? How big of a house did we really need.? I agreed we would really have to make a lot of changes in our lives if we married. We put the idea on a back burner.

We decided it would be best to just continue dating and get to know each other better. Time would help us work out these issues. A few more months passed, and Benjamin came to a place where he was ready to talk marriage. As we discussed some possible answers to our emerging questions, I decided I really did not want to make any major changes. I was pretty comfortable in my routine. So once again we decided together it was best to wait a while yet.

When we finally reached a point where we both felt God wanted us to marry, and we were both ready, we set a wedding date one year away. We remained in our separate houses. The only major change made was that Benjamin and Robyn started attending the church that the kids and I were going to.

Together we worked on our wedding plans. Benjamin made announcements and bulletins. We wrote the vows together. It was very important to us that our children were part of the ceremony too. Most important to both of us was that each person that attended our wedding had a personal invitation to know the Lord first hand. We wanted everyone to know what He had done for us. We kept the ceremony simple and sweet in that little church. We had around one hundred family and friends attend. My dad, Kendrick, walked me down the aisle. Our relationship was slowly starting to heal. Clifford was unable to attend. Kendrick also paid for all the food, and his sister cooked it. I made the flower arrangements out of silk flowers that my mom had purchased and fresh lilacs.

Chapter 35

We spent our honeymoon at an old Victorian bed and breakfast. Benjamin suggested this town because it was where he went to college. It was a great way to start our marriage, a week together with no worries, no chores, and just time to enjoy each other.

When we returned and collected up all the kids we decided that taking the kids camping would be a great way for us all to bond. So that is what we did for the rest of the summer. We had some really good experiences and learned a lot of Minnesota history and geographical beauty. Of course there were times where things were not running so smoothly, mosquitoes, poison oak, and sibling rivalry all had to be dealt with. Benjamin and I were always figuring out ways to assist the children in getting along.

I think Robyn had the hardest time adjusting, and I couldn't blame her. She had had her dad, the whole house, which included her own playroom and a cat, a parrot, and a rabbit all to herself for over five years. Now she had to share all of it with four more people and one more cat. The playroom became the boys' room. She no longer had her own bedroom; she now had to share with a three-year-old. Those were some big changes. With four children we had to come up with house rules, something else that Robyn had to adapt to. Everyone had to adjust and give.

Chapter 36

Just a few weeks after the wedding I received a phone call from Maxine, my step-mom's sister and she said, "Your dad just died in my living room." She told me the whole story about how he had a heart attack, and her husband did CPR immediately, but it was too late. I was stunned and did not know what to do. I began to tremble and cry. I told her to call me back and let me know what to do.

I did not hear from her the rest of the day so the next day I called her. I think she was in shock herself. She said, "There's nothing! He lost everything! There is nothing left!"

I was not sure how to take that and wondered if she thought I wanted an inheritance or money. I did not know what to say so I just said, "Let me know what I can do to help and what gets decided."

The following day she called me and said, "We would like to send the body to you, and you can have him buried." I told her I could not afford that. I had just gotten remarried, and I could not expect my new husband to pay for a funeral.

She said, "Okay," and hung up. I never did find out if they had a funeral, buried my dad, or had him cremated.

That same summer we received a legal notice in the mail informing us that we had to meet at a lawyer's office. Robyn's mom wanted to see her more often; we figured it was just a ploy to try to stir something up with our marriage. Together we decided not to hire a lawyer at this time but to just go see what would happen. I had really prayed about this and hoped we could call her bluff.

The day came to meet at the lawyer's office. Laura had a boyfriend there who was much older than she, and when he began saying that he was the one going to foot the bill to fly Robyn to his home in California and another in Illinois, Benjamin stopped him and said, "Who are you? You should not be making any of these decisions, as you may not even be in the picture next week." The guy pretty much kept quiet after that.

Then the lawyer asked Laura what she wanted, and she said, "I want my daughter every other weekend, every other holiday and half the summer.

We said, "That sounds great; let's get out a calendar and mark it all down." I think she was shocked that we did not argue with her. You could tell she just wanted to fight. We marked all the dates on a calendar. The lawyer wrote them all down to make a legal contract. We did have to negotiate some of the holidays and make it clear that every time we visited Benjamin's family that Robyn did not have to see her mother, but overall it went pretty smoothly.

When we got home we told Robyn and marked a calendar specifically for her with all the dates her mother was supposed to get her. She was pretty happy about the whole thing. She was ecstatic when her mother actually came and picked her up a few weeks later. The visit did not go too well, as Robyn argued with her sisters and ended up stepping on something sharp in the yard that lodged up in the bottom of her foot. She had to go to the emergency room and have it removed and stitches put in. She called us crying and just wanted to come home. Her mother arrived with a different boyfriend when she dropped Robyn off.

Laura did not call for weeks. The days agreed upon came and went without even a call. As each colored day on the calendar slipped by with no visits Robyn was hurt a little deeper. These disappointments caused Robyn to disconnect even further from her mother, but it did not cause her to get any closer to me, the woman she had to share her dad with.

Chapter 37

In the fall my kids started the school year in a new town with a whole new group of students. Jonathon probably had it the easiest, as he was just starting middle school, where kids from all different schools were being melded together. The building was actually the old high school that I had attended my freshman year.

Robyn began fourth grade and Dillon went into third grade, even though he was four days older than she. I had not sent him to school until he turned six. Benjamin had sent Robyn the year she turned five; she was ready for it, and so was he with his work load. Rachel went to preschool at the college while I took more courses. We quickly settled into a routine, creating family rules, holding family meetings, and trying to learn how to live in a house full of six people.

My kids did not see their dad as often as they wanted to. He had remarried days after our divorce. From what he told me his new wife had already moved out but had left her three teenage children with him. He would call me to ask for advice on what to do with them. One was habitually truant, another on drugs, and the third was giving him trouble. I had a hard time offering him much sympathy since it was a choice he had made.

Dillon always dreamed of moving back with his dad and talked about it often. Benjamin and I committed to each other that we would spend time together every morning before he left for work, every evening after dinner and a date night a week. Having this time to regularly communicate really helped build our relationship and work through some rough spots.

I think the honeymoon pretty much lasted until Christmas, my least favorite time of the year. We had our first big disagreement over the

Christmas tree. I wanted it to be freshly cut, covered in homemade ornaments and tinsel, with and angel on top. Benjamin's idea of the perfect tree was fake, glass balls for ornaments, garland, and a star on top. I am not sure why it made me so mad, but I was furious when he set the tree up that way. Benjamin tried to appease me and went out and got a fresh one, but it ended up losing most of its needles with in a few days, fueling Benjamin's reason for preferring an artificial tree.

I'm not sure how we eventually settled that one, but we did realize that we needed to come up with some traditions of our own. We tried to celebrate all the holidays with each of our families. It was just too hard to travel all over the state, usually in snowy weather. We had to come up with a plan that would work for everyone. Knowing that the kids would be with their other parent every other year, we decided it was best to celebrate every other holiday with each family. So when my kids were with their dad we would go to Benjamin's folks, and when Robyn was gone with her mom we would go to my mom's house.

We stayed busy that winter by going snowshoeing, taking the kids sledding, going to a ski-flying event and a huge annual winter festival held in our area every February. I also enjoyed decorating the house, painting rooms, adding trim, carpet and just making the 1930s house into a home.

Chapter 38

In May 1994 I completed my classes and received an associates degree with honors from the college. My mom, her husband, Sid, Benjamin, and the four kids all attended. I was happy to be the first college graduate in my family, and I knew Benjamin was very proud of me.

We had made plans to spend the summer camping all over the state, so that is what we did. We would arrive at a campground on a Sunday evening, set up camp and enjoy the week getting to know the area. On Friday we would pack up, go home do the laundry, get the mail, restock the groceries, mow the lawn, pack back up, and head out again. I always dreamed of living out in the wilderness as a kid, so this was a dream come true for me.

I wanted to go on with my education in the fall; there was no college nearby that had the program I wanted, so I started working on my bachelor's degree through an extended-degree program. Rachel started kindergarten, and I began to volunteer in my children's classes.

It did not take long to realize that with six people in one house we needed a second bathroom. Plans were made for a carpenter to come stay with us, add a bathroom in the basement, and remodel the one upstairs. That took up most of the winter but was well worth the time and money we put into it, plus we had a great time getting to know him better. He enjoyed doing homework with the kids, having dinner with such lively conversations, and keeping the wood stove filled during the night.

The classes I was working on were very intense: art, communications and psychology. I was really able to extract a lot of great information out of my college classes, especially those in my communication classes. The lessons gave me ideas to discuss with Benjamin. It also gave me the tools needed to analyze some of our situations and communications patterns. Things were not always going smoothly; the term "blended family" was not the correct word for what we were experiencing. We decided it was more like a tossed salad with parts and bits of each person being pushed and pulled in many directions.

It took a while to get our parenting styles melded together, but we eventually reached a place where we pretty much agreed to disagree in some areas, came up with compromises in others, and actually agreed in others.

The boys gave us static because they each wanted their own room, escalating the sibling rivalry. I was unhappy with the girls sharing a room, especially with the big age difference between them. We really had to work things out daily. We used weekly meetings and behavior and chore charts, reading every book we could get our hands on about blended families. When things were not running smoothly, kids bickering, meals not ready, messes everywhere, I would feel like just giving up and leaving, yet I knew that Benjamin was a great husband, and most of all God wanted us to be together.

With my newly learned skills from my classes I was able to analyze not only my wardrobe but how we sat at the dining room table as a family. I learned things about how our living room was arranged and how our different personalities saw things. I was amazed to find out that when I said dinner will be at five o'clock, meaning anywhere between four forty-five and five-fifteen, Robyn thought that meant at exactly five o'clock. It really helped me understand each of their personalities much better and change my way of presenting things to them so we could try to get on the same page.

Doing research in these areas helped me become a better communicator. It also helped me examine more closely how my upbringing made me what I was and what areas I needed to change.

One of my most rewarding assignments was one in which I had to analyze and write a paper on my three most intimate relationships using several reference books to support it. I really did not have to think hard to figure out who those three were, but I was not sure how I would communicate it to my professor. With God's help I was able to do it in a way that actually ministered to my professor. She noted on top of the paper "A wonderful piece of writing. This is a fine demonstration that we do not need to choose between feeling deeply and thinking deeply. I really enjoyed your paper!" She also wrote, "This is an unusual choice but one that makes a great deal of sense where there is the close and intimate interaction with one's Savior." Here are a few excerpts from the paper I wrote:

> The three people in my life that best fulfill my concepts and needs for intimacy are: my Savior Jesus Christ, my husband Benjamin, and my closest friend Sophie.... It is very clear that all people need support regardless of their care-giving activities.
>
> Each of these people fulfill different roles in my life by offering support in different ways. Jesus supports my spiritual needs by always being with me, guiding me and answering my prayers.
>
> Benjamin supports my physical, emotional and financial needs by being my friend, lover, help-mate, and provider.
>
> Sophie supports my emotional needs by listening, understanding, and sharing. She also supports my spiritual needs by praying for me and with me.
>
> My intimacy with Jesus can be defined as a feeling of closeness beyond comprehension. He knows me better than I know myself. He knows the number of hairs on my head (Matthew 10:30), and he knows the number of tears that I have cried (Psalm 56:8). I don't even know that about myself. Our intimacy involves commitment, one in which I can choose to

believe in Him or not and one in which he has promised, "I will never leave you or forsake you" (Hebrews 13:5).

On the above paragraph the professor added a note: "This is the crux of intimacy between any two entities."

In all three relationships we love each other. The components of love, based on Rubin's conceptualization are: attachment, caring, and intimacy.... I am always in Christ's presence (Psalm 140:13), and he is always in mine (1 Corinthians 6:19). It is a fullness of joy (Psalm 16:11) and peace that can not come from anywhere else. There is a desire for approval, to be cared for, and to be fulfilled by the other. These are all components of intimate love. "Therefore if there is any consolation in Christ, if any comfort of love, if any fellowship of the Spirit, if any affection and mercy, fulfill my joy by being like minded, having the same love, being of one accord, of one mind" (Philippians 2:1-2). This shows the attachment part of intimacy and love in my relationship with Christ.

Our relationship has many of the characteristics of intimacy that Davis and Todd identify in love relationships. Christ and I are friends. John 15:15 says, "No longer do I call you servants, for a servant does not know what his master is doing; but I have called you friends, for all things that I heard from My father I have made known to you." There is enjoyment, acceptance, trust, respect, assistance, confiding, understanding and spontaneity in our relationship. (John 14:23: "If anyone loves Me, he will keep My word; and My Father will love him, and We will come to him and make Our home with him.")

There is a type of passion that does not include a sexual desire but does include the elements of fascination and exclusiveness that I would describe with the scripture John

15:4: "Abide, in Me, and I in you. As the branch cannot bear fruit of itself, unless it abides in the vine, neither can you unless you abide in Me."

Christ is the epitome of caring. He gave his utmost (Galatians 1:4: "...who gave Himself for our sins that He might deliver us from this present evil age, according to the will of our God and Father.") I care for him by obeying his commandments and showing love and mercy to others." (John 14:15: "If you love Me, keep my commandments. 1 John 3:16: "By this we know love, because He laid down His life for us. And we also ought to lay down our lives for the brethren.")

Christ is an advocate between God and me. (1 John 2:1: "And if anyone sins, we have an Advocate with the Father, Jesus Christ the righteous").

Here is what the professor wrote next: "This is the first time any student has included a theistic relationship in this assignment. You have done it very well, not only in personal terms but also in terms of meeting the academic intent."

I went on to talk about my relationships with Benjamin and Sophie for several pages, but I want to focus here on my relationship with Christ. So on page seven I continued with this:

When I was young I did not think I had anything in common with Jesus. He was almost mythical, a person who once lived on earth in history and who was sitting in heaven watching me to see all the things I did wrong so He could punish me. When I was in my twenties I found out this was untrue and that we do have a lot in common. Hebrews 4:15: "We don't have a high priest who is out of touch with our reality. He's been through weakness and testing, experienced it all—all but the sin." Hebrews 5:7: "While He lived on earth, anticipating death,

Jesus cried out in pain and wept in sorrow as he offered up priestly prayers to God." God became human in Christ so that he could understand our frailty, become our friend by having our humanness in common."

Getting to know someone is a never-ending task, largely because people are constantly changing, and the methods we used to obtain information are often imprecise." (Knapp) In all three of these relationships we are continually getting to "know" each other better and to love each other more. We, do this by spending time together, talking, sharing fun times and a variety of experiences....

With Christ I spend time reading the Bible, talking to him in prayer, and listening for his still small voice within my spirit. As I acknowledge that Christ lives in my heart by faith I am able to comprehend and experience the width and length and depth and height—to know the love of Christ that passes knowledge, that fills me with all the fullness of God (Ephesians 3:17-19). How can you get any more intimate than that? "For Jesus doesn't change—yesterday, today, tomorrow, He's always totally himself." (Hebrews 13:8)

The professor's note said, "Though I direct my communication to His Father I share your sense of closeness and comfort!" The last part of the paper had to do with how will you alter your intimate communications to enhance each of these relationships.

After explaining what I will do with Benjamin and Sophie I added: "In my relationship with Jesus Christ I need to be more consistently obedient to his voice, enter into his rest, and show His love to others."

I ended the paper with, "In every relationship I will have throughout my life I will need to continue to hone my listening skills by being more empathic, supportive, flexible, and interactive."

Chapter 39

It was a hard decision and there were several events leading up to switching churches. The most important reason was to have a place that was "our" church. Robyn felt like she had to leave "her" church, and my kids had "their" church. Benjamin suggested that we try a church that was of Four Square Denomination thirty miles from the house. I knew it was the right move when the first time we visited Dillon looked up at me and said, "Mom, you know the way your mouth feels when you get your teeth cleaned at the dentist? That's how this church makes me feel on the inside."

We weren't married very long when I began having very intense pains in my right side on a pretty regular basis. Every once in a while it would bother me enough to go to the doctor. I usually would have an ultrasound or some other test, the doctor would tell me, "You don't have gall stones so you will be fine."

I tried my best to stand on faith, daily quoting healing scriptures, seeing a Christian nutritionist, several kinds of fasts and cleanses but all to no avail; the pain continued to haunt me. By the winter of 1997 I could not stand it any longer and got a recommendation from my doctor to go to St. Paul and see a surgeon.

Benjamin took me to the appointment, and within minutes of meeting the surgeon he set me up for a special test that measured how well my gall bladder emptied. Within an hour we learned my gall bladder was not functioning correctly, and I would need surgery before Christmas. I asked if I could wait a couple weeks so I could attend the kid's holiday concerts. It was fine with him.

It was an out-patient procedure, and I came home that evening. Benjamin's folks stayed with the kids after school until we returned home from the hospital.

During the following year we stayed busy volunteering and parenting in many avenues together and separately; Boy Scouts, Christian Coalition, Parent Network, Fifth-Grade Fun Day, dance chaperones, the list goes on. Together we continued parenting our children, visits to the orthodontist, cheering at sporting events, parent-teacher conferences, attending church functions. We kept our daily and weekly commitment to spend quality time together, too.

Chapter 40

One day while I was volunteering in Rachel's first-grade class the teacher asked me if I wanted to be put on the list for subbing. I could get paid for doing what I was already doing for free; that sounded like a good deal to me. I just need to be available when a para-professional aid was unable to come to work. I was unsure if I qualified, but she assured me that I only needed a high-school diploma. I already had an associates degree and was working on my bachelor's degree. I went to the district office, did all the paper work, and was officially added to the list. I received jobs almost daily. I continued with my studies, because my goal was to graduate from college before Jonathon finished high school in 2000.

In October Lily invited me to go to Minneapolis with her for a weekend retreat. I was so excited to learn that my very favorite Christian musician would be playing for the conference. Grace, a friend from church, and Mari, Lily's foster daughter, joined us for the journey.

The whole weekend was heavenly; we knew God was present. We were amazed to find the hotel right downtown without any problems. We were unsure where exactly the conference was. We started carrying our stuff into this enormous hotel with no idea where to go. A young man, around twelve years old, saw our confusion walked up to us and asked if he could help. He happened to be helping at the event and showed us right where to go immediately.

The greatest thing for me was that it was such a small group and we actually got to hang out with many renowned Christians or spouses there of and a few other semi-famous people. It was so much fun talking with, taking pictures of, and getting autographs from individuals that were known for their relationships with Christ. The individual classes were great, but one of the most memorable lessons was that I was supposed to start a journal about my life so far, then to ask the Lord how He saw each event. The example he used was when a lady was so very sad about miscarrying her baby the Lord showed her that the baby entered heaven that day. The very next week I started writing parts of my life story in a journal so God could use my life's journey to show others what He had done for me.

Grace and I have always hit it off from the first time we met. I think it is a combination of our musical tastes (we both like many of the same musicians and other contemporary praise music), we are the same age, both Christians, and have psychology backgrounds. As our friendship grew and we were able to get to know each other even better we realized that we had more in common than we thought. We both had three biological kids, each near the same ages, our husbands were the same age and went to the same college at the same time, and Jesus had delivered us both from some of the same things in our past, mostly looking for love in all the wrong places.

Dillon, my middle child, continued to pester me about moving back to Otter Bay with his dad. I spent so many hours crying and praying over this situation that a day arrived that I finally felt a peace to let him go. It still hurt, and I felt like Abraham when God asked him to offer up Issac as a sacrifice and to totally trust God to take care of him. So halfway through the school year Dillon moved sixteen miles from me into that old decrepit house, to a place with no rules and little supervision. It may have been a twelve-year-old's dream, but it was a nightmare to me.

That year had a very rough conclusion, too. My mom found out she had ovarian cancer and needed surgery right away, plus my brother Brody and his wife Jennifer began divorce proceedings. Even thought they had six children together, by this time they were ready to head in separate directions.

My mom's surgery went well, but she was so very nervous she did not want to be alone, she wanted me to stay with her all of the time. I wanted to support her any way I could, although it was hard on me to be away from home. Benjamin was very good about taking care of the kids. My work schedule was very flexible, so I could go spend a few days in Cedarfield. I was allowed to stay right in the hospital with my mom, sleeping in her room for the couple days as she recovered. The surgeon was able to remove all the cancer, and she did not need any kind of treatments afterward.

My brother's problems did not go away that quickly. When we visited for Christmas I brought the two youngest girls to our home and had them stay with us until mid January. I invited Brody up, and he would bring all six kids for the weekend. Other times I would make a quick trip to Cedarfield and bring at least two of them home with me to give Brody a break.

That spring I had discovered lumps in my breast. After what I had been through with my mom and step-mom I made sure to take care of it right away. I did have them checked by a gynecologist and then by the surgeon who had removed my gallbladder; he said it was just fibrocystic breast disease, but to keep an eye on it and come back in six months.

I heard about a test going on in Marshfield where they were experimenting with some anti-cancer drugs for breast cancer. I called and got an appointment in June to see if I qualified. I had to bring my previous mammograms along. After I went through numerous questions and was examined, the doctors became very concerned, as the lumps had a hardened area that had grown since the mammogram. I was rushed into a surgery room and had ten biopsies. I was very sore but happy to learn it was not cancerous.

We did get to do a little camping that summer with the girls. In July we were heading to Benjamin's brother's to camp with them on the other side of the state. We called him on the cell phone to say we were getting near their house.

He said, "Your family has been trying to get a hold of you; your dad had a heart attack. I quickly called down to Cedarfield to find out what was happening. He needed a quadruple heart by-pass surgery first thing in the morning.

At this point in my life I had forgiven my dad but still did not have a lot of warm, fuzzy feelings toward him, God was preparing to change that, too. I had learned; to love Christ is to follow His commandments and one of those commandments is to honor your mother and father. It was a very hard on us to discontinue with our camping plans and drive all the way across the state to Cedarfield for the surgery. We knew the right thing to do was to go, so we got some rest and then took off early in the morning. We did not get there before Dad went in for surgery. My brother, his ex-wife, my mom, her husband, and Dad's brother and cousin were all there waiting when we arrived. He pulled through just fine and was very happy to see that we had made it there for him. This added more healing balm to our relationship.

We were able to camp a bit more that summer, but soon we were back into our autumn routine.

Chapter 41

In the fall I applied for a job as a toddler-coordinator at the Children's Museum. I had been on the original board for creating the museum and had done volunteering there. I did get the job and was able to use it as part of my studies toward my degree. I also became a photo-organizing consultant, mostly because I wanted to create albums for each of my children so they could remember the good things about their life.

On a spiritual level I had several life transforming experiences during this time. I was able to attend a conference, where I saw the preacher lady I had only seen on TV before. I had become a partner and faithful watcher of her program ever since Lily introduced me to her show. Getting up at five-thirty almost every week day morning to learn how to enjoy my life on a much deeper level from this great woman of faith. The atmosphere of being with thousands of believers for praise and worship, teaching and learning was magnificent.

One night during the conference I laid on the floor in my sleeping bag attempting to sleep. I'm not sure if I actually fell asleep, but I had a dream-like experience. In it I was standing in a bathtub taking a shower. Warm liquid was flowing out of the shower head penetrating and absorbing into my body like water does to a sponge. As I looked at the liquid it was not water but blood, I realized it was the precious blood of our Lord Jesus. That deep life cleansing penetrated my soul that night. I felt the mark of being a bastard child, the bruises of my childhood, the scar of loneliness, the dirtiness of being raped, the stain of being an unwed mother, the blemish of divorce, the stigma of being on welfare and the fear of rejection wash down the drain never to return. I realized this supply is endless, that the past is washed away. I am His child. A paradigm shift occurred within me that is very hard to put into words.

I had become a leader for a prayer group that prays for our children and school once a week. The national organization was having a meeting in Minnesota, so I asked Grace if she wanted to come along. She wanted to get a group going in her home town, so together we attended the conference. The speaker was related to one of the moms whose child was killed in a school shooting. It was very touching and motivating to keep our groups going and to pray for our schools. It was also a great way to get to know Grace better and be encouraged by her testimony.

In December I received my diploma for my bachelor's degree in the mail. I also ordered a class ring from the college. I had always wanted a high school ring but was unable to get one; this was even better.

Life seemed to be going pretty smoothly. I was helping with my brother's kids whenever possible, I was done with schooling, and it felt great to take a break from all those studies. I continued subbing in the school district, helping the elderly neighbors with doctor appointments, taking care of a teenage handicapped boy, and enjoying visits from my son Dillon.

Chapter 42

In January 2000 my heartbeat became very irregular and was making my body jump like a hiccup every third heartbeat. I ended up in the hospital emergency room being prodded and poked until they decided I was not having a heart attack and whatever was happening was most likely not fatal. During the next few weeks I wore a monitor, started seeing a cardiologist, had many more tests. The cardiologist tried several different medications to get my heartbeat under control. Finally it was decided that I had an electrical problem with my heart. This caused the left ventricle to close too fast. Finally a medicine was found to keep the arrhythmia at a minimum, but I still needed to see a cardiologist regularly.

While all this was going on with my heart I applied for my substitute-teaching certificate, and received it. I also continued to work as much as possible.

One day when I was sub teaching in a school that had the Internet I had an idea to type in my biological brother's name. I had been wondering about him ever since Raquel had mentioned that he existed. My mom had also clued me in a little about him by sending me newspaper obituaries whenever any of his relatives passed away. I was happily surprised to actually find an address and phone number.

I wasn't really sure what to do, but then I decided to write him a letter explaining who I was and see what would happen. A few weeks later when the letter returned in the mail, I was crushed, and really wondered why God had let me find the address in the first place. Then I remembered that I still had a phone number. I decided it wouldn't hurt to call the number and see what would happen. I was pretty nervous, but when I got an answering machine, the man on the recorder had a Minnesota accent, and it was in Maine so I figured it had to be him. It was hard to comprehend this could be my flesh-and-blood half-brother. I left a short message to please call me and my number.

Two days passed, and no call was returned. I called the number several times just to hear his voice but did not leave another message until the third day. Minutes after the second message was left, my phone began to ring. It was Jeremiah calling me back. He told me who he was. Nervously I asked him if Clifford was his dad, and he replied, "To the best of my knowledge."

I said, "Well, he was my dad, too."

The mix of emotions that came are hard to explain it was such an excitement of knowing he really existed mixed with the possibility of knowing he could reject me that I don't even know that there are words to explain it. We awkwardly talked a few more minutes and he promised to get in touch with me in the future. He did explain that he never answered his phone because of telemarketers and because of some of the weird calls he would get from people that have read his books.

The very next week I went out and bought a computer and connection package so I could correspond with him via the Internet. After checking out his website and letting him know I now had e-mail we began writing to each other a couple times a month. I printed out and kept every e-mail he sent me. It was so nice to get to know each other a little bit.

In May we drove up to the campus for my graduation ceremony. It was awesome to be in such a large auditorium with so many people. We were briefed on where to walk and what to do. I was a bit hurt than no one from my family came to watch. Benjamin's family made up for it, though; not only did Benjamin and Robyn come, but Benjamin's folks, sister, her husband, and three children. Benjamin's sister touched my heart when she ran up to me during the procession and handed me a dozen roses. Most important to me, though, was that two weeks later I watched my firstborn graduate from high school. What an emotional experience to know that my baby was all grown up and ready to be on his own.

In June we received a letter that we needed to be in court on the day of our seventh wedding anniversary, and it was about child support. At this appearance we were told that since Natasha was now nineteen, and we had one child (Robyn) and his ex-wife had one, we no longer had to pay child support. What a wonderful anniversary gift! Wow, did we feel God had really intervened on our behalf! Benjamin's knees actually kept buckling under as we walked home from court that day; we were ecstatic.

Our summer went as usual, with our camping although only the girls came along. Jonathon had moved to Cedarfield to work with my brother Brody. Dillon was still living with his dad.

Chapter 43

Late in the summer Jeremiah asked me in one of his e-mails if I had ever heard of a place called "Camp Thunder Moon."

I replied, of course I did; my kids went to summer camp there. I cleaned a house nearby and would be attending a ladies retreat there in the fall. He was doing a seminar in California and had gotten hired to teach a course at the camp here in Minnesota. I was ecstatic; we began making plans for when he and his wife would come.

To add to all the excitement we decided that without any child support payments we could afford a new vehicle. I started doing research on the best vehicle for us and we settled on a mid-size SUV. The ironic part was the day all the paper work got signed was the exact date of my divorce eight years earlier.

Jeremiah and his wife Abigail arrived the first week of October on a Sunday afternoon. I spent the whole day anticipating their arrival and was so excited when they finally pulled in I could hardly contain myself. When I was thirty-nine years old my brother and I were meeting for the very first time.

We learned so much about each other that day; we found out we are exactly two months apart to the day. Our spouses are also two months apart to the day, only they are five years older than us.

He brought his photo albums along so he could share his whole life with me. His mom was very happy for us. I shared my photo albums and was able to show him photos of our father, whom he had never met. They spent the night at our house, and then the next day I showed them how to get to the camp so they could settle in there for a few days.

I was excited because I was allowed to attend his classes. I had received permission from the camp director the week before. He teaches non-competitive group games, and I was able to join right in with the group; it was wonderful in a dream-come-true kind of way.

After the morning session we had lunch together where I learned he was a vegetarian and eats very similarly to me. At the camp they always say grace before a meal. It was neat to be praying with my brother so soon after meeting. Another really cool thing that happened was that a gal who did not know us walked up and asked if we were twins. We both began to laugh and said, "Not twins, but we are siblings who just met yesterday."

I took many photos and just relished in our time together. After Jeremiah and Abigail taught at the camp a few days they came back to our house to spend the evening, we went out to a nice restaurant and had a wonderful time getting to know each other even more. The more we discovered about each other the more similar we found out we were. What a great nature/nurture study we could make.

On the way home from dinner that night our new vehicle rolled over its first one-thousand miles, and as we exited the vehicle, the Northern Lights were out in full force. That just put the icing on the cake. It was as if God was putting on a display just for us. Abigail was very amazed to see the Aurora Borealis. She had never seen such a spectacular display in the heavens before.

The next day it was very hard to see them leave, but knowing that we now had a true bond between us we would stay in touch, and I knew we would be able to grow closer as time went by.

At the end of October my dad, Kendrick, found a great deal on a slightly used truck. He called Ben and asked if he wanted to buy a nice pick-up truck for a good price. Benjamin had been driving a car that a friend from work had given him for one dollar. We called it the LaBomba because it was such a big old boat. Benjamin figured it would fit into our budget now that we were not paying child support, so we got the loan and all the papers and license taken care of.

Ironically all of that was completed on November first, the anniversary of Benjamin's divorce ten years prior. Only God could have lined up all these dates; they could not have happened by chance.

Chapter 44

Brody had found a great gal and was excited to get married again in the spring. His new wife Sarah attended the same church as he, so her two children knew Brody's six kids. I was glad I made it to the wedding; it was very nice.

Summer was filled with our usual camping trips, but come August I was in miserable pain again. It was very similar to what I had experienced in the past when my gall bladder was bad. I dreaded going to doctors again, but I was determined not to let this type of pain continue for a long time.

I started going through a battery of tests right away, colonoscopy, endoscopy, etc., and nothing was showing up as a reason for the pain. Seeing how much pain I was in the surgeon admitted me to the hospital for more tests. I became very sick from the narcotics, so they gave me anti-nausea medication which I ended up having an allergic reaction to. The longer I was in the hospital the worse I became. The team of doctors was starting to think it was a blood clot in my liver or kidney, or something to do with a birth defect in my kidney. It was not affecting the functioning, but it had an extra renal pelvis; it was very elongated, plus it created a kink in my ureter. Nothing was showing up in any tests. I was absolutely miserable and begged them to just let me go home. I began wishing and praying that I could just die.

During this time Benjamin and I discussed having some medical check ups for him. His right arm had been twitching and moving on its own since he was teen. He had been through very intensive and painful tests when it all started. The medical team determined that he had a calcium deposit on his brain. As we talked about it we realized it had been over twenty years since it had been looked at. Hoping that there may be some type of medical treatment to make it go away, he started having tests performed. After having a MRI and a MRA the doctors sent him to Duluth for further testing.

We spent one whole day at the hospital preparing Benjamin for some invasive test. It is such an intensive test they needed to make sure his body could handle it. Late in the afternoon we met with a neurosurgeon who told us that after the test the next day we would have six weeks to decide what kind of brain surgery Benjamin would have. He thoroughly explained the five options and then sent us onto a movement specialist. We talked to this doctor for a while. The phone rang while we were in the room. It was the brain surgeon. He told the doctor that he started looking more closely at Benjamin's records and decided to cancel the scheduled test. The doctor was upset and said, "You shouldn't have done that; he needs the test."

The surgeon said, "No, I am sure it is not vascular or anything that can be fixed with surgery; it most definitely is a calcium deposit."

The movement specialist said, "Come back tomorrow and we will discuss this some more."

We had some pretty bittersweet emotions. It was nice to know Benjamin would not need an extensive brain surgery but hard to swallow that there was nothing they could do for him.

At the visit with the movement specialist the second day we learned many more details about what was going on in Benjamin's brain. It is called hemichorea. This calcium deposit in his brain causes his right side to move in a dystonic fashion. We also learned how BOTOX injections could calm his arm down for three months at a time. He started the treatments right away. Even though Benjamin could barely stand the sight of a needle he kept himself calm for forty to sixty pokes.

Over the next few weeks I had even more tests, and the surgeon decided it would be best to just go in and do exploratory surgery, so on October 31 I went in. The doctor removed my appendix and looked around but did not find anything that he could see that would cause that much pain.

I was happy to be able to go home that day. I was determined not to let anything ruin any more of my days, so four days later we went to a Vikings game.

Chapter 45

The year 2002 was probably the year that was the least eventful compared to the rest. Robyn graduated from high school in June and made plans to attend the college where I went and then go on to be a physical education teacher.

Our cat, Caddie, who was seventeen years old, died. This was much harder on me than I expected. After I thought about it a while I realized why it hurt so deeply: he came from Grandma's farm. She was my ex-husband's grandmother, to whom I had been really close.

We filled that summer with camping and bike riding. We actually clocked over five-hundred miles on our bikes. We also went rafting on the Minnesota River.

In June I attended a scrapbook convention in Minneapolis, and while I was gone my friend Sophie had called Benjamin to see what he thought about me taking a trip to New York City with her. He was fine with it but promised Sophie not to say anything to me. I was not home fifteen minutes when Sophie called and asked if I would fly to New York City with her and her handicapped daughter at the end of August. It took me about fifteen minutes to make up my mind; I quickly called her back, and the plans began.

I won't get into all the details here, but it was the trip of a life time. Benjamin's best friend, Daniel, who lives in New Jersey, picked us up and made sure we saw everything. He had driven taxis in NYC when he was younger, so he really knew his way around. The greatest highlights for me were Ellis Island, as it reconnected me to my grandpa, the boat tour around the whole island, attending *The Lion King* on Broadway, Times Square Church for a Sunday service and for the wedding, Ground Zero, the Empire State Building, and the list could go on and on. I have two photo albums filled from the trip.

Several weeks after returning I noticed that I was getting a urinary tract infection, something that seems to happen frequently with me. I asked Benjamin to run me to the emergency room so I could get on antibiotics right away. Well, a hour or two after we got there a young doctor comes in and says, "We can't give you any strong antibiotics because your pregnancy test came out positive."

I said, "That is impossible!

The medical staff started treating me like a person in denial and tried to keep me calm." They told me to get into the obstetrician as soon as possible. I demanded they take the test again, so they did, and it came out positive again. This whole time Benjamin was out in the waiting room, and I did not want him to think I was pregnant, especially after what he had been through with his first wife. I knew I was not pregnant, so I said, "Please take a blood test."

They said, "We will, but you need to go home and get your rest; we will call you with the results tonight." They did call around eleven p.m. and admitted that the results were negative; I was not pregnant.

As the week went on a problem developed because the antibiotics were too low a dose; the infection got worse, and a horrible pain developed in my back. This was pretty much that same area that I had the pain in earlier during the gall bladder attacks. The medical team did an emergency ultrasound on me, but once again nothing could be seen to explain the pain.

I was not going to mess around with this, so I called my surgeon, ninety minutes away. He said I should come right down; he knew I had a very high pain threshold, and if I was in that much pain something had to be wrong. He thought it might be my back muscles, so he shot some steroids into me and sent me home. He called the next day, and I let him know that it did not help. I told him there was no improvement, so he said I better get to my urologist right away and have my kidney checked.

My urologist figured that my kidney had dropped, but the problem would not show up when I lay down to have the test. He made sure that it was done standing up and lying down. My kidney was dropping nearly 5.4 centimeters and was pinching my ureter off in two places. I had the pain of a kidney stone, times two. The very next day I was put under so the urologist could put a stent between my kidney and bladder. This relieved the majority of the pain but it was still very uncomfortable. The doctor explained that I needed very extensive kidney surgery called a nephropexy that would hold my kidney back up in place. He set the date up for the end of January.

Robyn decided college was not what she wanted to do, so she dropped out. She did not make this decision until the day after the cut off where you could get your money back. My dad had paid for most of it, since we did not have enough money for college tuition. I felt bad that we were unable to pay him back. We were disappointed with her choice but knew she had to figure out for herself what she wanted to do with her life.

Next she decided to join the Marines like several of her classmates had done. She went through the process and was accepted. They were unable to give her a starting date, so she was in a delayed enlistment program until they could get her in. She decided to get a temporary job as a check-out clerk in the local grocery store. We had the family Christmas celebrations at our house instead of going out of town. Everyone in Ben's family came to see her before she took off for boot camp. She ended up getting fired on Christmas Day. She wasn't too worried because she would be leaving soon.

The urologist performed the operation. He told Benjamin and me before hand that he would start the incision at my belly button, and depending on if he could reach my kidney from the front or not he would determine where the incision would end. It could go all the way around to my spine, and then my back rib would have to be removed. He would not know until he was doing the surgery.

My mom, her husband, Sid, and Benjamin accompanied me to the hospital that day. They had the hard part, waiting, while I was sleeping in surgery.

When I woke up I was sick from the narcotics, still on oxygen, catheter and an intravenous. The first thing I saw was a beautiful bouquet of flowers from the teachers where I subbed. I then found out that the incision only went from my belly button to my hip. I needed to lie still for three days with those pressure socks on to prevent blood clots. I was sick to my stomach most of the time.

Finally the day time came to remove the oxygen and then the catheter. I panicked as I realized I was going to have to stand up and really feel the pain on the incision area. After having help from the nurses with the first few walks, pushing through the pain I was able to get up and walk around myself. The nurses let me know that the more I walked the sooner I would recover so I walked as much as possible.

Once home I was unable to lift over five pounds or drive for six weeks. During this time I was in quite a bit of pain. I took minimum amounts of pain pills and spent most of my time in the word, listening to praise music, resting and letting my body heal. My friends and family visited often.

While I was healing Robyn was not around the house much during the day. She slept at the house and ate most of her meals in our kitchen. She was terribly messy and left a trail every time she went through the house. This irritated me and it put a lot of static between Benjamin and me. I tried very hard to bite my tongue, knowing she would be leaving soon for the Marines, but it was very difficult.

Then a day arrived that she needed to talk to Benjamin and me. She was crying and it was obvious something was really upsetting her. She then broke the news to us; she was pregnant and would be having a baby in October. This so reminded me of my life it really flooded me with some emotions that were overwhelming. I was afraid that the baby's father would abandon him like Jonathon's father had; I was concerned that he would be ostracized as a bastard child like I was, and I didn't know if Robyn was ready for such a huge responsibility.

I attended the annual ladies retreat in March, sponsored by our church. Many women prayed for me, and I did a lot of crying over the pain, both physically and emotionally. The Lord assured me He would give me the strength to make it through.

I was offered a long-term subbing job for the rest of the school year in a position that I liked to do, so I took the job. It not only got me out of the house, it gave me a break from Robyn, who refused to work or help around the house.

Benjamin and I discussed thoroughly what would be best for the whole situation and came to the conclusion that in the spring he would have to give Robyn an ultimatum. She would have to start paying rent or get out. She chose to leave and move in with the baby's father. She visited our home often but was not making messes all over the house and could not get in if we were not home; this took a huge strain off of our marriage.

We also experienced a true "God Moment" during this time. One morning on my way to work I ran through the car wash. Before I did I removed the magnetic signs for my business off the car doors. After the car was clean I put them on and drove the twenty miles to work.

After work that day I was very tired and did not want to cook so Benjamin said, "Let's go out." As we exited the car to enter the building we noticed that one of the signs was missing from the passenger door. Benjamin was a bit irritated because he knew I spent a lot of money for those. He said when we are done eating, "Let's just run up to the school and look for it."

I was tired and said, "No, I will just look for it on my way to work in the morning." He insisted we go; I was pretty mad and would not even talk with him. He drove us the whole twenty miles there, turned around in the school parking lot, and there was no sign anywhere. I had pretty much decided it was gone and wanted to say something about all the time and gas we had just wasted, but as we pulled out of the school road to the highway, a car went by in the opposite direction with my sign attached to the front of it, just in front of the wheel well. Benjamin quickly turned our vehicle around and went after the other car. He passed it honking and waving. The guy pulled over and

Benjamin grabbed my sign off of the car, the guy said he had found it on the road and was going to take it home and cut it up. Benjamin just thanked him and returned to the vehicle. If we had been there only seconds before or after we would have never got that sign back. We both knew God had his hand in the whole thing.

At the end of May Dillon graduated from Otter Bay High School, although he had already completed four semesters of college through a special program. He had also joined the Air Force, and we saw him off at the Minneapolis Airport in May.

At the beginning of June I had promised Pearl, a friend of mine from work, that I would walk on her Relay for Life team in August. I was so proud of her, as she was a four-time cancer survivor and was happily back at work making the best of each day. It was hard for me to change those plans, but when I found out I could see Dillon graduate from boot camp I had to make a hard decision. The graduation ceremony was set up for the same week as the walk. I called Pearl and asked if she would mind if I took a rain check for the following year. She completely understood.

I went to a local travel agent and made the reservations for Rachel and me. We flew to San Antonio together; it was really exciting for Rachel to fly and for me to watch her be on her first jet. She had only flown once in her life and that was in a little four-seater for a fourth-grade field trip. The trip there went well, but I was nervous about driving around San Antonio and being able to find the places that we needed to get to.

My first hurdle was when I picked up the rental car; I had to decide if I needed to get the extra insurance or not. Next I had to be able to follow the instructions to find the base. I was very thankful that it was rush hour, and there was a lot of construction going on, which meant the traffic was only moving at thirty-five miles per hour. It was very easy to find the base. We went right to the front gate, showed our identification, and went to the BMT Reception Center to wait for Dillon. We somehow miscommunicated and were unable to connect that evening, but we were able to find out many of the details we needed for the following day.

We had to find the hotel that the travel agent had booked. It ended up just being a little over a mile away. I was ever so thankful to get to the motel.

The next morning we attended a ninety-minute briefing before we were bussed to the parade grounds where the graduation would take place. There were no seats left in the bleachers that were filled with thousands of people, so we had to stand out in the blazing sun. After thirty minutes of recognitions and announcements, the band started to play, marching toward us with all the squadrons following behind.

At the briefing we had learned that Dillon's unit was behind the flag bearers, so it did not take long to spot him in his blues, even with over one thousand other soldiers. Words can not describe the pride and joy I felt.

As the flights stood at attention, the moment came when it was announced, "Find your airman." Rachel and I were able to run right up to Dillon. I gave him a hug, and he was able to leave his group and head to the bus with us. He gave us a tour of the area he had called home for the past six weeks. We toured the base, which is a small town all its own. He had to be in his barracks by 1600 hours so we left him at 6:00.

The following day we picked him up and went downtown to the Riverwalk, the Alamo, and the Mall. I prayed out loud quite a bit while driving, which caused both the kids to tease me as they were not used to seeing me so nervous. I was hoping Dillon would be able to do the driving, but that was against Air Force policy. We went to IHOP (International House of Pancakes) for dinner, and had him back on time. The next day we were only allowed to visit a few short hours, so we stayed on base and went into the museums, a mall, and outdoor airplane display called Bomb Run. It was very hard to say goodbye because he was shipping out to another part of Texas for more training early the next day. We did not know when we would see him again.

Our last morning Rachel and I packed up and headed to Sea World. After a couple of wrong turns we finally found our way there. I felt pressed for time because I did not want to miss our plane, and I had no idea how long it would take to get to the airport. We picked out the most important things to see and do first, feeding the seals, petting the dolphins, viewing the penguin house. We were even able to fit in The Shamu Show. Rachel really wanted to feed the dolphins, but we would have had to wait another hour until feeding time, and I did not want to be late. Rachel was unhappy with me.

After asking several people for directions to the airport I thought I understood where to go and headed in the direction I thought I was told. We came to a red light and stopped. As we were waiting for the light to change a lady in a bright-yellow car pulled up on the right side and motioned to have Rachel roll down her window. The lady hollered, "Your brake lights are not working."

I said, "Thanks. It is a rental, and we are heading to the airport right now."

She said, "No, you are going the wrong way." We sat through a full green light and another red light as she gave me instructions on how to get to the airport, and no one showed up behind us. She said, "Oh, it's too complicated. Just follow me, and when I go left on Culebra Street you go right."

So I followed her several miles through residential areas, and when she stopped to turn left she put her hand out the sunroof, pointed right, and waved good-bye. We entered Hwy 410 and arrived at the car-rental place in minutes. We were shuttled to the airport and ended up a couple hours early. I have no doubt God sent that woman to show me the direction to go that day. The whole trip was very blessed and a dream come true, since joining the Air Force and being at Lakeland Air Force Base was something I wanted to do with my life but never got the chance. Seeing my son do it was a great reward.

Chapter 46

We did not camp that summer except for the Church camp out at the end of August, but we did bike ride and go to the cabin quite often. In the fall I took another long-term subbing job in the same type of position I had before, but in a different building for a different teacher, and it was only fifteen miles away. I worked that job straight through until Thanksgiving break. It was much more stressful.

On October 19 Jack and Robyn went to the hospital, believing that Robyn was in labor. The hospital staff was going to send her home, as it seemed as if the labor had stopped, but on the morning of the twentieth her water broke, so they stayed. We were in contact throughout the day, but Benjamin and I both had to work. In the late afternoon we took Rachel up there, and finally at 7:55 p.m. Lance Benjamin came into this world, 7 lbs. 1 oz., 19½ in. long, exactly on his due date. It was love at first sight. He crawled right into my heart, and I have all the grandma pictures to prove it. His birth also did a great healing in my relationship with Robyn. I always say that I went from being the "wicked step-mother" to being the "queen of motherhood" that day.

My dad, always willing to help wherever he can, brought Robyn and Lance home from the hospital, since the rest of us were working. Robyn showed signs of post-partum depression so I would sometimes just go over and get Lance and bring him to our house so Robyn would get out of bed and move around. Within a couple weeks they were able to find another place to live. I watched the baby while Ben helped them move.

Not only did becoming a grandma do something to me inside, it also made me want to be sure I would be around for a long time. I was already getting frustrated that my weight was slowly creeping up. I was discontent with the fall weather and not being able to get out bike riding and hiking, so I made a decision to join a 30-minute workout program for women. It has made staying in shape doable, keeps me healthy, and it is a great place for good social interaction with women from all walks of life.

Dillon surprised me at Christmas time when he came home on leave. Shortly after the holidays he completed his military training and moved to Cedarfield. Since he is in the Air Force Reserves he only goes in for training one weekend a month and two full weeks a year.

At one of Lance's check ups we asked his pediatrician her opinion on his baby car seat. It had been used. The doctor said it was not a wise idea to ever use a previously owned car seat; she would advise that we get a new one a soon as possible.

We went directly to the store, and I bought a new seat for him. Benjamin put it all together in the evening making sure everything was snug and safe. Soon we were to find out that that was another God moment in our lives; within a few weeks the seat was put to the test. Benjamin was at work and received a frantic call from Robyn, she stated, "We were just in an accident and are going to the hospital by ambulance." Then the phone disconnected. We did not know at the time that the battery had fallen out.

A few more minutes passed, and she called back to tell Benjamin what town they were in and what hospital they would be at. Benjamin called me at work to figure out how we could get there the quickest. We met in Heron Creek and raced to Agate Falls to find out what had happened.

Robyn had been driving straight through an intersection on a green light. A newly licensed driver was driving toward them. The young driver made a left hand turn directly into them. Both vehicles were totaled.

Robyn was burned from the speed of the airbag when it inflated. Jack had been knocked unconscious from hitting his head on the windshield. He was buckled in, but his height of six feet nine was his worst enemy. Lance was oblivious to the whole thing and just remained his happy self, even during the transport to the hospital via an ambulance. All three were released after being examined, and other than some bruises came out with no major injuries.

I found out about a police officer who specializes in children's car seats. I made arrangements to have her inspect the new seat and she informed me that the car seat was now unsafe because there is no way to tell what kind of damage was done to the straps. We were happy to buy another seat, as we realized that he could have been severely injured or worse if he had been in the old seat. God was truly protecting them.

Chapter 47

In the spring of 2004 Benjamin and I started a new hobby called geocaching. A friend told me about this great sport, and I knew it would be something we would both really enjoy doing. Since we would not be able to go far from home with Rachel working, it would be a way to get out in the woods and still be home in the evenings.

The game is played world wide and was made possible when the President made it legal for citizens to own a Global Positioning System Receiver. A GPSR gets signals from satellites revolving around the earth letting the holder of the unit know exactly where in the world they are using longitude and latitude numbers.

To play the game one must go to the website www:// geocaching.com and plug in the zip code for where they live. The site then pops up all the caches that have been hidden near that area. Then you go out and find the cache. A cache is a waterproof container that can be made from a variety of different sizes but usually an ammunition can or plastic box. Within this box, that is hidden on public land after going through an approval process, is a log book and trade goods. Trade goods are usually trinkets, coins, toys, tools, or any small object that someone might like to take home with them, the only rule is that for every one you take you leave something of equal or more value. The log book is for signing and telling others about your adventure and what you think of the cache. You also go back on line and log that information on the Internet.

This hobby engulfed our summer with so many great adventures and learning opportunities we can write a whole book about them. We both feel that nature is God's way of displaying His splendor, and geocaching is just one way to go out and enjoy that splendor and be refreshed by His spirit.

In June of 2004 I was able to make good with my promise to Pearl, and I walked in the Relay for Life with hundreds of survivors and supporters. Being able to represent my loved ones who have been killed by this ugly disease, support my friend, walk with Margie, Sophie, and several friends from the school was very touching.

We filled the rest of the summer with visits to the cabin, playing board games with Benjamin's folks, enjoying our hobby of geocaching. We started taking Marty, the handicapped adult we take care of, on many of these adventures. It is a hobby he truly enjoys, too.

I felt I had reached a point in my life where I was experiencing real contentment and happiness something that I had been searching for, for a long time. I now know this peace can only come from God as there is nothing else that can give this type of still knowing in your soul. I also began asking God what my purpose in life is. Why had He created me?

In September I took a long weekend trip to Kansas City, Missouri with Sophie and Jewel to visit her daughter and two granddaughters. It was a wonderful trip. We visited some really nice places like the Bridges of Madison County, an apple/pumpkin farm, Steamship Arabia, and we even attended my first opera. Overall, a very enjoyable trip.

The last Monday of June Robyn let us know that she and Jack had decided to get married on Friday. They planned on a very small wedding in a lawyer's office. She did not even plan to wear anything but a tee-shirt and jeans, but I insisted on her wearing a dress of mine. I also purchased some flowers for them, to make it special. When the time actually came for the ceremony Robyn wanted Rachel to be a witness, but she was not old enough, so I ended up being a witness, the photographer, and babysitter.

We helped them move into a different house, this one with two bedrooms, a full basement, living room, dining room, deck, and a great yard. Ironically it was right down the street from the resort where I lived as a teenager.

We really filled our summer with fun geocaching excursions all over Minnesota, the Upper Peninsula of Michigan and even a little bit into Wisconsin. We have many photos and albums full of memories that will last a lifetime.

As the fall came upon us we started to get back into our routine. When I went to one of my regular appointments with my urologist we discussed that I had quite a leakage problem. Even though I was receiving regular but very painful dilations it did nothing for the problem. After several tests it was decided that I needed a sling placed under my bladder, that was dropping. At the end of October I went through the procedure and had it fixed in an out-patient surgery that has successfully fixed the problem.

The next year seemed to start out fairly well the kids seemed to all be heading in worthwhile directions, and our parents were healthy. Jonathon completed an apprenticeship and is a plumber, and Dillon was busy with a variety of jobs.

In March 2006 my aunt Kendrick's sister Juliana, who had been on dialysis for some time, went in to have some surgery on her wrists. A few days later, while she was having some physical therapy, she had a stroke that landed her in the hospital. During the night she pulled a tube partially out, and it ended up contaminating her body and putting her into a coma. After several days the family decided to pull the life support, and Aunt Juliana passed on.

I went to the funeral, a three-hour drive away, to support my dad and see my cousins. At the luncheon after the service I was talking with one of my cousins when my cell phone rang. It was Rachel in a panic, just hysterical. She wailed, "My dad just died!"

I had her explain what had happened. She said she was called to the office at school and told she had a phone call. She picked up the phone, and her Aunt Terese informed her that her dad just died, they thought it was his heart. She asked me to call the boys. I went into a slow-motion mode. I called each of the boys. Then I called Rachel several times to make sure she had some support. I felt so helpless being so far away. I told my parents and my cousins and headed back home as quickly as possible.

The next few days was a whirlwind of activity. Benjamin and I had just redone the floors with a wood laminate, but the trim was not up so that had to be completed. The boys came. I had to make meals, arrange where the kids would stay, and be supportive yet stand back and not get in the way: it was a hard line to balance.

I did not stay for the original consultation for figuring out the funeral. I left when the kids' grandparents, aunt, uncles, and their dad's latest girlfriend came.

After the meeting Rachel and I went and ordered flowers and went shopping for clothes to wear for the wake and the funeral. While doing that we also checked at the courthouse to find out if he had divorced or had an annulment from his third wife, but according to their records he was still married.

I went through my photos to help Rachel make up a couple picture boards. The boys went to a house where their dad had been living and cleaned out all his possessions. Dillon brought several loads of laundry in; I told him that I would wash the clothes that their dad needed to wear in the casket, but I would not do the rest of his laundry. The boys were okay with that.

Rachel and I brought Ivan's clothes over the next day. The funeral director very nicely informed me that the papers had not been signed. If the contract was not signed the body would have to be taken some place else. I had advised the boys not to sign it, that their dad's third wife, girlfriend, or other family members should take care of it. I asked if I could see the contract and if anything could be changed, but there wasn't. I called the boys over, and after a few tense moments, they signed the contract, promising to pay several thousand dollars for the funeral with a minimum payment of one-hundred dollars a month. I gave them credit for taking on such an huge responsibility at such a young age.

Rachel and I returned to the funeral home around three o'clock to drop off the photo boards. We were able to view his body. This was so very hard on Rachel; I just wanted to wash her pain away. We stood there and cried together.

Benjamin went over with us early for the wake. Jonathon quickly asked him where to stand, what to say and do. I saw a real healing between those two that weekend. Jonathon borrowed some of Benjamin's clothes. It was nice seeing them have real conversations on an adult level. I spent the evening of the wake staying over to the side so that people could come over by me if they wanted to. It was very awkward, but I had to be there for my kids. I was amazed at how many did come over and talk to me, too.

I was saddened to learn that neither of the boys had a very good last conversation with their dad; I knew they were dealing with many issues on different levels. Rachel had not seen him in over a year, and that was at her cousin's funeral. This was not by my or Rachel's choice but by Ivan's. Plus, how many kids have to bury their parent and pay for a funeral out of their pocket? My heart was broken over my kid's pain. Benjamin comforted me, and a peace came that it all would work out.

My mom, her husband, and my dad sat with me at the funeral and the meal after. Even my friend who I had met in the hospital when Jonathon was born came to offer sympathy. It was comforting to have them with me.

I had such an overwhelming sense of God's provision during this whole ordeal. I had a deep knowing that God had allowed me to go through all the pain of the divorce so that he could take care of me. I could barely imagine where I would have been if we had still been in that marriage. I would be a widow now. He had died suddenly with no insurance, no money, no property, nothing but debt. I would have never earned my college education, would have never gotten out of a life of poverty, and would have had to go back to some type of low-paying, back-breaking work like waitressing or house cleaning again. I was so thankful where the Lord had me now. He is so faithful.

My mom has always stayed in contact with a few of my biological father's family. At Aunt Juliana's funeral she had given me a folder full of photos and family genealogy information about my family. With all the chaos of the funerals I had laid it a side and did not get to look at it. One day I rediscovered it and found out that a first cousin had left her phone number and address in it. I called her, and we connected, deciding it would be great if we could meet in person. So that is what we did, we met in Cedarfield at my mom's, and then a few weeks later she and her husband came up and spent a day with us.

When the fall rolled in after a summer of fun and relaxation, we got back in to our routine again; I was very happy. I knew that now that we had a new computer I had to write out my life story and that I needed to make it a priority. In October I felt celebratory that I had made it a full year without any surgeries and so happy to feel healthy and content.

The first week of November I received a call from my cardiologist's office that said I needed to take a medicine because my routine blood test said my potassium was too low. I started back on the diuretic. I was tested a short time after and received another call that I needed to add some prescription potassium. After more time and yet another blood test I was to add magnesium. A few weeks later the nurse called to tell me to double each of the medicines. I was not happy. I believe in doing things as natural as possible and taking as few medications as possible. Then a few weeks later a scheduler called and informed me that the cardiologist was sending me to a nephrologist. After six medicine changes there was little change to my potassium level. At that point I did not even know what a nephrologist was, so I asked the gal who had called, and she said it is a dialysis specialist. I asked her why I had to see one of those and she said she had no idea; she was just a scheduler.

My brother Jeremiah and his wife Abigail came in early November for a week visit. We had a wonderful time just being together. I was excited to teach them how to geocache. We played games, shared stories and photographs. At the end of the visit it was so hard to see them go. I started to cry, and Jeremiah suggested that Benjamin and I come out to Arizona for a visit. I thought it would be a great idea. I had wanted to visit the area ever since I had left years ago.

A couple weeks after they left Sophie, her daughters, granddaughter, and I went to a special event at my church. It was a pre-Christmas event where we met many local authors. I talked to quite a few and found out about different publishers. One of the authors really shared some details and told me she was very happy with a particular company. This reminded me about my testimony project that was saved on the computer, and planted a seed to look into it some day.

Benjamin went in for his routine dental check-up and found out he had an infected abscess and needed a root canal, which was done on December first. While Benjamin was getting that taken care of I saw the kidney specialist, who relieved my worries by letting me know I did not need to have dialysis. He did not feel my potassium was something that was too abnormal or that there was anything wrong with my kidneys, but he did run many tests to make sure.

During this time I started having flank pain similar to that when my kidney dropped. After many tests from the nephrologist and from my regular physician, also a trip to the emergency room with inconclusive results I was sent to a specialist, who figured out that a nerve was encapsulated in scar tissue from the kidney surgery, causing all surrounding nerves and muscles that run along my bottom ribs front and back to spasm. They calmed it down with steroid shots.

The first week of January we also found out that Benjamin's mom had a pretty serious heart condition; she needed to get on a few different types of medications, and she needed to start seeing a cardiologist.

If this wasn't enough stress we also learned that my dad needed two heart valves replaced. The second week of January I took him to the cardiologist for a full heart catheterization. His diabetes was so out of control they almost canceled the procedure. With insulin they got him at a safe enough level to check out how extensive the heart valve damage was. The good news was that only one valve needed to be replaced. It also helped him understand that he needed to monitor his blood sugar and watch what he eats.

His surgery was scheduled for the end of January. I rearranged my life and made sure not to take any subbing jobs. Then a few days later he called me and said he wasn't having the surgery; he was convinced they just wanted his insurance and money. He canceled the surgery. Then he started having shortness of breath and a heaviness in his chest. I took him back to the doctor a couple weeks later. The cardiologist really took the time explaining that the normal valve size is three centimeters and his was about one half of that, which means it is severely damaged. After thinking it over for a few days he rescheduled for February.

Benjamin was voicing some concern about some testicle pain he was having as he thought he might have a hernia. We kind of ignored it for a while, although he brought it up once in a while.

I saw the gynecologist, and she thought I had a polyp, so she removed it. A week later I found out that it was not a polyp but a cervical cyst. That was removed immediately, and it tested as being benign. I also visited the cardiologist in January to discuss what was going on, and he explained to me that my potassium level should be above 4.5 and that mine was dropping to 3.1. He also felt that if I dropped below three it could be fatal, with the heart arrhythmia.

Benjamin's pain became bothersome enough to go see a doctor. A physical exam was inconclusive, so an ultrasound was set up for February. The physicians assistant also had him take a PSA test, simple blood test that he had not had before.

The end of January came, and the doctor called and said that Benjamin's PSA was elevated and that he needed some biopsies. He said this could not wait, and he was to get in on Friday at four o'clock for the procedure. This did not sound good, but we really did not understand what it meant.

That Friday evening the doctor did twelve biopsies on his prostate. We were told that we should check in the next Tuesday when we come back in for the ultrasound. That Tuesday took its time arriving, but finally it was time for Benjamin to have the ultrasound. We also visited with a regular physician for a check up, since Benjamin had not had one in six years.

A colonoscopy was scheduled for March and a fasting blood lab for Monday. Next we went to the urology department to see if results were in and what the doctor thought of the ultrasound. The nurse who took care of Benjamin during the biopsies slipped out to the waiting room and whispered, "The results were positive. The doctor will be busy for another hour or so, go get something to eat and come back at four o'clock."

Benjamin said, "What did she say?"

I told him, "She just said you have cancer." We just sat there in shock. Neither Benjamin nor I had really let the thought of cancer cross our minds. We were sure it was a hernia or calcium deposit. We exercise, eat right and take care of our bodies. How could it be cancer?

When we saw the doctor at four o'clock he took over an hour to explain all the options and risks, he was very thorough. The testicle pain had absolutely nothing to do with this; it was just from vascectomy staples. We feel it was God's way of getting him to the doctor.

The good news we learned was that the cancer was in the first stage. On the aggressiveness scale that goes from one to ten his was a six. He would recommend full removal of the prostate and cancer.

I started to create two altered books to help deal with the emotions and thoughts going on. It took days to finally hear when the appointment with the doctor would be to set up the surgery. I took out books from the library, ordered some off the Internet and read on many cancer websites. Doing so much research we were both relieved to find out that everything we read agreed that surgery was the best answer for Ben's situation.

Finally on February eighth a message was left on our machine that Benjamin's appointment was set up for four o'clock on the twentieth. I had retrieved that message from our answering machine while I was working. I almost broke down crying when I realized it was the same day as my dad's surgery. I wanted to be there for Dad's surgery and planned on being his caregiver after. I did not think it would be physically possible to be in both places, since they were over one-hundred miles apart.

On Monday, February nineteenth, I took my dad to Spruceburg, ninety minutes from home, and we checked into a motel. During the evening a friend of his, her family, and my brother Brody showed up. Needless to say I did not get any sleep that night. We were at the hospital before five in the morning.

Dad was prepped and we said our goodbyes. The medical staff took Dad from us. We sat in the waiting room. I stayed until ten-thirty. I had to head home for Benjamin's appointment, staying in touch with my brother via the cell phone the rest of the day and evening.

Benjamin met me at home at noon, and we did a few things to pass a little time. At three o'clock we were just heading out the door and the phone rang. It was the clinic, and the gal said that Benjamin's appointment would have to be postponed. The doctor was just called into emergency surgery. It was a devastating blow. We felt like we had been holding our breath for two weeks. We were ready to start breathing again. We needed a plan in place and now we were going to have to wait for only God knew how long. I just went to bed exhausted.

I was thankful that the clinic called back the very next day. I was not happy when she informed us that we could not see the doctor until the end of February. We stayed busy teaching, trying to make the time pass. I dealt with a lot of my emotions by working in those two altered books.

Two days after dad's surgery I went down to Spruceburg to visit him. I was amazed that he was already up and walking around. It was nice spending time with Brody; we were able to spend some time together and share our hearts and love of God. It took Dad a few days to decide where he was going to go when he would be discharged. He was hoping to be in his own home and have me help him out. He realized that it would be impossible now, with Benjamin needing surgery. So he decided to go to his friend's house near Cedarfield.

The day finally arrived for Ben and me to meet with the surgeon/urologist. He took over an hour explaining the whole procedure to us, and apologized for the last appointment being canceled. He answered all of our questions, and we told him that we agreed that surgery was the best way to go.

The doctor could not give us a date for the surgery at that point but assured us that his office was to call us soon with that information. His best guess was that it would probably take place late in April but maybe as late as the end of May. We did not find out until March thirteenth that the surgery would be performed on April tenth.

My dad recovered quickly. We talked on the phone almost daily. He started checking his blood sugar and using insulin. He did rehab and has lost most of the excess weight.

April tenth finally arrived. The laproscopic prostectomy took seven and one-half hours. Benjamin's folks stayed with me during the whole surgery. I had access to a computer with Internet during the process so I stayed in contact with many friends and relatives, who were in continuous prayer during the whole process.

The procedure was a success. Other than some nausea that first night Benjamin did great and was able to come home the very next day. It took us a while to get the hang of dealing with the catheter, but after nine days of healing the catheter was removed.

We went home, packed our suitcases, and went on a three-day weekend at a Bed and Breakfast with twelve other couples from our church. We geocached the whole weekend, driving, hiking, and just enjoying life, happy to know that God is in control and the cancer is gone. Benjamin went back to work full time the following Monday.

Rachel moved out and bought a car, getting a loan all by herself with no co-signer during this time. I was not very happy with these decisions, but I knew she was just exercising her independence. It really stressed me out emotionally, so to help myself deal with it I completely redecorated her old room. As I ripped each layer of wallpaper down and recalled each of the paint colors underneath. I could bring back good memories: the sky blue of the room when it was Robyn's playroom, the jungle green from when the boys shared the room, the lavender that I surprised Rachel with. As I wondered if I was a very good mom, the Holy Spirit reminded me that I was the very best mom I could be and did the best job I could. I knew it was good to move on and take time to look for some good things about an empty nest.

I saw that the house stayed clean, especially the tub and sink. There were always leftovers to eat, and I did not have to cook if I did not want to. I also knew that Rachel's and my friendship had entered another level, one that is more adult like, a friendship strengthened by mother-daughter ties. I was very proud of her for earning two scholarships and two awards at the awards-night ceremony at the high school, keeping her grades up and making mostly mature life choices.

May was filled with doctor appointments for Benjamin and his mom. We also spent much time planning a trip out West to visit my brother Jeremiah in Arizona, Holly and her family in the Quad Cities, and Benjamin's brother and family in southern Minnesota. The summer was filled with many wonderful travels; great memories were made, and loved ones reconnected with.

Benjamin has had four check-ups since his surgery, and his PSA has been declining as expected. They will not declare him medically cancer free until two years have passed, but we know that all the cancer is gone.

My baby, Rachel, graduated from high school and is attending college. Her plan is to become a lawyer.

The second week of September I was able to attend a Christian Women's Conference in Saint Paul. I went with three gals from my church, whom I have done several Bible studies with. We had a delightful time learning how to enjoy everyday life, how to apply God's word to our life's every day, how to grow spiritually stronger each day by spending time with God in His Word ,and most of all to walk in forgiveness. The praise and worship was heavenly. I felt like I climbed up another level, getting a wee bit closer to heaven.

A few days after the conference a friend's home-schooled daughter called me and asked, "Do you know where I could get a book published?"

I dug out the information I had collected at the Authors Day and told her where to go on the Internet. I decided to go on the site and look around myself. I wondered if my manuscript was far enough to send in. I thought I would try to figure out how to do it and messed around trying to attach it to an e-mail. The code that I needed to fill in to prove I was not a computer had my birthday, 620 in the middle of it. I took that as a sign from God to do it. It went through. I was surprised that I got a confirmation e-mail; it had been received right away. A few days later I was e-mailed a contract. I had to make a decision.

I contacted the author who had used this publisher before, and she was still very happy with them. I started to get wet feet worried I would hurt my family members by sharing such intimate details of my life. That morning I picked up a devotional and read: "Jesus said, 'Follow me.'" The author went on to explain that no matter what anyone else thinks, you need to do what God is asking you.

Several friends have encouraged me to do this. Then I was reading an article in a Christian women's magazine titled, "God Is Calling You to Great Works" that stated that God is using women to carry out His plan on earth. She said that God is calling an innumerable company of women today to bear the good news of the gospel. She based this on Psalm 68:11 (AMP): "The Lord gives the word [of power]; the women who bear and publish [the news] are a great host." This confirmed to me to embrace my purpose in life, and that is to share with others what God has done for me.

God continues to amaze me. I was just reminded by a friend that when Jesus hung on the cross it was very humiliating, but He obeyed. I want you the reader to know that Jesus really loves you and wants you to come and commune with Him, now and forever. I pray that you will find that abiding joy that is so deep that there is no circumstance or problem that can shake it. I know that whatever you go through Jesus will be there to hold your hand, if you let Him, He will be with you through it all.

Printed in the United States
104979LV00001B/124/P